MYSTERY MAGNET

THE LAST PICKS BOOK 1

GREGORY ASHE

H&B

Mystery Magnet

Copyright © 2024 Gregory Ashe

Published by Hodgkin & Blount

https://www.hodgkinandblount.com/

contact@hodgkinandblount.com

Published 2024

Printed in the United States of America

Version 1.05

Trade Paperback ISBN: 978-1-63621-080-3

eBook ISBN: 978-1-63621-079-7

CHAPTER 1

"Do you like puzzles?"

I resettled my glasses and managed, "Um, yes?"

Okay, maybe not the strongest answer in what was *technically* a job interview. But cut me some slack; I had a lot going against me. In the first place, I was talking to Vivienne Carver. The Vivienne Carver. In the second place, I was operating on zero sleep because my cross-country drive had taken longer than I expected. I'd covered the last hundred miles that morning in a bleary-eyed sprint to reach this little town on the Oregon Coast. And third, in spite of everything that had happened, I was still (apparently) the same old Dash.

Which was why the next words out of my mouth were "Actually, yes. I mean, definitely." The words were like a freight train; I couldn't stop them as I blurted, "In fact, I love puzzles."

Vivienne's eyebrows went up. She looked like she does on TV, in case you're wondering. And in the author photo on her dust jackets. She was blond, like a lot of women of a certain age, her hair a medium length and layered and curled and styled until it was the size of a basketball. A red sweater—classic Vivienne. A pair of cheaters hung on a chain around her neck, but it was hard to imagine she needed them, because her eyes were a startlingly intense blue. She had great skin. Wrinkles, sure, but she could have passed for twenty years younger.

All right, ten.

"I think puzzles are the heart of a mystery novel," she said. "Don't you?"

"Well," I said, "yes."

Vivienne opened her mouth.

I tried to stop myself, I really did. But it was another blurt: "And no."

Vivienne closed her mouth.

"But mostly yes," I said. "I mean, yes. Absolutely. The heart of a mystery novel."

She opened her mouth again.

Sometimes, being Dashiell Dawson Dane was like being in a horror movie: you knew you weren't supposed to go down into the basement alone to check the circuit breaker, or you knew you weren't supposed to get freaky with the rude but cute jock in the backseat of his car at Make-out Point, or (just for the sake of example) you knew you weren't supposed to keep talking. But you just. couldn't. help yourself.

"It's just—the puzzle," I said, "and the human element."

Vivienne closed her mouth again. Her eyes really were stunning. That was, apparently, the kind of thing I could think while I was having an out-of-body experience.

But then she smiled and said, "Quite right, Dashiell. That's well put. The puzzle and the human element. Very well put. Not that I would expect any less from you. I read 'Murder on the Emerald Express.' It was very clever. Quite the send-up of Christie, I think."

"Thank you."

"And your parents, of course."

And there it was. The whole reason I was here. Not because I'd written a couple of short stories that had eventually landed in *Black Mask* and *Flying Aces.* But because I was the son of Patricia Lockley (*Mommy's Sleeping* and *Blind Furies* and *What the Laundress Saw*) and Jonny Dane (the Talon Maverick series). Because, to put it bluntly, Vivienne was doing her colleagues a favor.

Not that I cared. At least, not too much. I needed to get away from Providence (and Hugo), and here I was—about as far as you could get.

"How are your parents?" Vivienne asked. "I haven't seen them in ages."

"They're all right."

"And what are they doing these days?"

"Oh, you know. Mom stays busy with the chickens, and Dad has his guns."

Vivienne laughed, and I tried to smile, fighting the familiar tightness in my chest.

"Portsmouth really is so charming," Vivienne murmured. "I've only been once, and your parents were such wonderful hosts. I'd love to see them again."

"I'm sure they'd be happy to have you visit." I dredged up another smile. "I hope you like skeet shooting."

That made her laugh again. She settled back into her chair—it was so massive that it was really more of a throne—and examined me more carefully. After a moment of that long, considering stare, I looked away. Her study, where we were having this interview, was exactly what a famous author's study should look like: a cavernous fireplace, built-in bookcases (filled with her own titles, of course—all the books in the Matron of Murder series, and translations into dozens of languages), a massive cherrywood desk. She had a laptop, a sleek little aluminum thing, but the typewriter that featured so prominently in the *Matron of Murder* TV adaptation still had pride of place. Posters from the show lined the walls. The actor they'd picked looked remarkably like Vivienne, even though the protagonist in the books, Genevieve Webster, was nominally fictional; I wondered if she'd had any say in the casting. Interspersed with the posters were photos of Vivienne. Vivienne with politicians. Vivienne with celebrities. Vivienne accepting honorary degrees and keys to various cities. Pictures of Vivienne when she'd been younger—glamorous, but not quite beautiful. Apparently, she owned (or had owned) a yacht.

"Tell me, Dashiell—"

"Just Dash." I rushed to add, "Unless you prefer Dashiell, that is."

She was silent for a beat. "Tell me about your writing, Dashiell."

"Well," I said. And that was as far as I got. That tightness in my chest worsened. "I'm very passionate—"

"Your ideas, Dashiell." She waved a hand. "Your plans. Yes, I understand that your position here will be as my administrative assistant. But we both know it's a bit more than that. You're a talented writer." She gestured to the desk, even though it was bare aside from the laptop and typewriter. "Your resume is impressive. You've attended top writing workshops. You've done some teaching yourself."

"Just as an adjunct."

"And you have publications."

"Two short stories."

"But good, Dashiell." She leaned forward. Her glasses swung on their chain. Her gaze seemed to spear me to my chair. "They're good stories. They're smart. Even better, they're true. I don't need to ask you about your references. I don't need to know that you can type and use a word processor and answer phone calls. I want to know who you are, and I think you know, Dashiell, that the way to know a writer, truly know them, is to know their stories. People lie all the time. But every story is an act of disclosure, no matter how hard we try otherwise." She waited, as though I might say something, and then sat back again. "So, let's hear them."

"Well," I said. I almost mentioned Will Gower. Vivienne genuinely seemed to want to know, and I'd lived with Will Gower in my head for so long, in all his various incarnations. But Phil, Mom and Dad's agent, had said no more Will Gower. He'd said I needed something high concept. Something with a hook. "I guess one of them is—have you seen *21 Jump Street*?" The silence grew until I said, "Like that. Only gayer."

Vivienne blinked. "That sounds...timely."

The words loosened something in my chest, and I sat forward, talking more easily now. "Oh, and do you know *Veronica Mars*? That's another idea. But make it, like, super gay."

"I see."

Excitement made me speak faster. "Or *Riverdale*. And I know what you're going to say, but yes, we can go gayer."

"Uh huh." For a moment, her face was blank. And then she gave a rueful grin. "Are you going to be terribly disappointed if I tell you I have no idea what you're talking about?"

Then she started to laugh, and for some reason, I found myself laughing too.

"I'm sorry," I said. "I can explain—"

"You'll explain later," she said, waving the words away. "I want to hear all about these ideas. I'm very impressed with what you've done, Dashiell. Very impressed. And I want to see more of it. You're very talented, and you're going to go on to do great things." She gave me a droll little smile. "And if I can offer a spot of advice here and there, well, I'd be happy to help however I can."

"Oh my God, that would be incredible. I—I've been struggling lately. With writing. Struggling to finish things. Struggling, um, to write anything, actually."

It was impossible to read her expression, but her voice was kind when she finally said, "I know a little something about that myself, believe it or not. We'll see if we can't shake something loose."

"That would be amazing."

"It would be friendly, Dashiell. This is a small town; being friendly is our way of life."

"I don't want you to think I expect you to, I don't know, do anything. You're busy, I understand that. And this is a job. I'm not asking for special treatment or favors or anything."

"I understand," she said gently. "And I'm telling you that I want to help you. I'm looking forward to it, actually. Life does get a little stale every once in a while. I believe you're going to be a breath of fresh air." Her pause had an unexpected quality to it—something I thought might be another kindness. "Your mother was distressed when she called me. I understand you made the decision to move rather suddenly."

"It might have seemed sudden to other people," I said. I fought to keep my voice easy and relaxed. "But I'd needed a change for a long time."

"I understand you've had some…difficulties lately."

Shaking my head, I said, "I'm fine. My parents are being dramatic."

Vivienne said nothing, but the raw intelligence of those blue eyes told me she didn't buy it. I waited for the thing I couldn't handle: questions about Hugo. Questions about why. The questions my parents had been asking for weeks.

I spoke first. "I promise, Mrs. Carver: I'm fine. The chance to work with you is an incredible opportunity. I'm excited to be here, and I promise, I'm not—" I almost said, *I'm not running away from anything*, but that would have been a lie. "—going to let you down."

In the distance, the surf crashed restlessly.

Then Vivienne nodded. "So, you'll take the job?"

A beat passed as I processed the words. "Yes, definitely, absolutely."

"Wonderful. We'll have some paperwork for you to sign later, of course. Non-disclosure agreements, tax forms, that kind of thing. Writing is a craft and an art, I don't need to tell you that, but it's also a business—most people are terribly disappointed when they learn that, but I'm sure it's something you learned growing up with your parents."

"I don't know if *they've* ever learned it," I said. The surge of relief at her offer—a job, a place to live, stability—was so great that the words slipped out before I could stop them. My face heated as I added, "They let their agent handle everything. And their accountant, I suppose."

"Then I see we have some work to do," Vivienne said as she came around the desk and took my arm. "If there's one thing I can teach you, it's business.

Now, let me give you a quick tour, and we'll get you settled. I bet you want to rest after your early start this morning."

"How did you—" I cut myself off and grinned. This was, after all, Vivienne Carver. "Okay, how did you know?"

"A hint of stubble; you don't have a heavy beard, but it's there. And you missed a button on your shirt."

I fumbled at my placket.

"And you did seem a bit flustered as you came up the drive, dear."

Groaning, I shook my head. A bit flustered was putting it mildly.

Vivienne patted my arm and laughed gently. "It's all right. We'll get you squared away in no time."

She hadn't been joking when she'd called it a quick tour. Hemlock House—Vivienne's cliffside manor (there really wasn't any other word for it)—was enormous, and it was old, too. Fireplaces in every room, damask wallpaper in deep hues of red and green and blue, wainscotting, polished wood floors covered by thick rugs. And God, so many crystal chandeliers. Heavy drapes framed the windows, and as we walked, I caught glimpses of the sea cliffs and, below them, the slate-green waters of the Pacific. The briny smell of the ocean was familiar and not at the same time. I'd grown up in a seaside town, but in a very different part of the world.

"Hemlock House was built by Nathaniel Blackwood," Vivienne said as we walked, her arm in mine. "He made a fortune in the late nineteenth century, fur and timber and agriculture, and—this will be your room, dear—" She opened a door, and I caught a glimpse of an enormous canopy bed, a secretary desk, an oil painting of a horse, and what looked like a very expensive clock. Then we moved on. "—and he retired here with his much, much younger bride."

"Some things never change," I said.

Vivienne laughed. "No, they don't. And I'm sure it won't surprise you to learn that Nathaniel Blackwood was, to put it mildly, an eccentric."

"The Howard Hughes of beaver pelts."

"Something like that. He spent years working on the plans for Hemlock House. Years, dear. And he was unbelievably exacting in the construction. Spent an absolute fortune building it, making sure everything was exactly as he'd dreamed, and then died shortly after it was finished. He fell from the balcony and died on the cliffs. His bride, as you might imagine, went on to live a long, happy life with a parade of lovers."

"He fell," I said. "Right."

Vivienne gave me that droll little smile again, but it faded as she said, "She died the same way, strangely enough. A fall from the balcony."

"So, no going out on the balconies. Check."

"She was pushed by a younger man. He claimed he didn't do it, of course, but everyone knew—there'd been fights about money, fights about other women. The bride never had any children, and the estate was a legal morass for decades. Finally, the house was sold to a private investor who went to great lengths to preserve the historic aspects. Most of the furniture is original, although there have been updates for modern conveniences." In a guilty whisper, she added, "I couldn't live without cable."

"I couldn't live without coffee."

A grand central staircase led down to the main floor, and when I say grand, I mean grand. Think, Disney castle grand: a sweeping spiral of polished marble, with a crystal chandelier hanging in the open well at the center. I'd come this way when I'd arrived, of course, but I'd been so nervous about the interview—if that conversation, in hindsight, could even be called an interview—that the details had registered only peripherally. Now I took it all in: the oil paintings in gilded frames (more horses), the black-and-white checkerboard tile (more marble), the unmistakable spaciousness of it all, as though the house had been built for giants. And, I noticed, the person lying on the floor, splayed out like a body at a crime scene.

"Uh—"

"That's Fox," Vivienne said. "Fox, this is Dashiell."

"Just Dash," I said apologetically.

Vivienne studied Fox for a moment and said, "They're doing something with the wallpaper. I have to admit I don't really understand it. How's it going Fox?"

Fox was stocky, their dark hair buzzed and sprinkled with silver; I put them somewhere in their forties. In their ankle boots and paisley vest, they looked like they were striking a balance between hipster and steampunk. Without raising their head, they said, "Terrible. It's a disaster, and everything's the worst, and I'm dead."

"They're very dramatic," Vivienne confided.

"I'm not being dramatic. This project was a huge mistake. I'll never be able to do it. I'm a fraud and a sham. My life is over."

"They're an artist," Vivienne said, and then, a bit more loudly, "And an *artiste*."

Fox moaned.

"Something with sea-glass," Vivienne said as we continued down the stairs. For a lady in her sixties, she was spry—I'd read an interview she'd done in *Ellery Queen*, and she'd talked about running and bicycling and, I kid you not, her beloved mini trampoline. "Fox is very successful."

"Not anymore," Fox said from the floor. "I'm a huckster. I'm done."

"Dashiell is going to be joining us at Hemlock House, Fox. Do you have any words of wisdom for him as he settles in at Hastings Rock?"

"Never love or cherish or hope for anything," Fox said in a broken voice. "Life is a trap."

"And they're ever so much fun at parties," Vivienne murmured as she led me across the hall. We passed through a pair of pocket doors into the living room. It had the biggest fireplace I'd seen yet, with a pristine marble surround, a tarnished overmantel mirror, and a decorative tile-work hearth. Shiny brass fireplace tools and a matching screen. Maybe it sounds like I'm spending too much time on this fireplace, but it was enormous. You could have driven a hearse through it.

Like the rest of the house, this room had those lovely details and decorative elements that marked it as a product of another time (and another socioeconomic class). Cornicing, ceiling roses, more of those dramatic crystal chandeliers. Tufted sofas in brocade and velvet flanked by wingback chairs of aged leather. Mahogany tables cluttered with brass and glass curios (a telescope, a miniature globe, a bowl). Tall windows, their curtains held open with tasseled tiebacks to let in more of the day's cloudy light. And, of course, bookcases. These weren't Vivienne's books. These looked like they'd come with the house, with beautiful bindings that had weathered the perpetual seaside damp surprisingly well. Interspersed with the books were botanical prints and porcelain figurines and glass cloches that held taxidermy birds.

"I know, dear," Vivienne said. "Barbaric. I couldn't sleep for a week the first time I saw them staring down at me. The dining room is through here."

Another set of doors carried us through the dining room (a ginormous table, paneled walls, and yes, a fireplace). Vivienne pointed to a door across from us and said, "That's the sun parlor." Then she headed for a second, smaller door that looked like it was designed to be unobtrusive. "And the kitchen is through here."

As she opened the door, a woman's voice rang out behind us: "Mrs. Carver!"

I turned to look, of course. Just like Vivienne. But before I did, I caught a glimpse of a butler's pantry immediately behind the door and, through the open doorway on the far side, the kitchen: patterned tile, cabinets with slate countertops, big sash windows, an island covered with butcher block. It looked updated in a way the rest of the house didn't, with the Thermador fridge and the Viking stove and the LED lights. But that was probably for the best—most people wouldn't enjoy actually working in a Victorian kitchen, with a table and a wood stove and a "kitchen dresser" (yes, I put it in quotes on purpose) instead of, you know, modern conveniences.

All of that passed through my mind in an instant, though, because what caught my attention was the boy and the woman.

The boy was a teenager, with long, dark hair and a deep tan. He was small, swallowed up in board shorts and a baggy tee that showed a crab riding a surfboard, but he had a wiry build that said he was stronger than he looked. His features suggested he might have Native American ancestry. He was staring at me with a look that straddled the line between startled and panicked.

The woman was older; she might have been close to Vivienne's age, maybe a few years younger. She had dark eyes and generous laugh lines, and her mane of thick hair had a shock of white in it that made me think of a witch. Her hand was on the boy's shoulder, and I couldn't tell if the pose was possessive or defensive. Her expression had a grim, locked-down quality, like a woman ready for a fight. She met my gaze for a long moment, and I was distantly aware of Vivienne saying something to whoever had called her name. And then, without a word, the woman gave the boy a push, and he darted away.

"—is Dashiell," Vivienne was saying. "He'll be working with me at Hemlock House." I turned around in time for her to say, "Dashiell, this is Millie."

I had a single instant to take in the woman in front of me: early twenties, blond, a wide mouth and a scattering of freckles. She looked like five feet of flyaways and what Hugo had once called *manic pixie energy.*

"Oh my God," she squealed as she hugged me. "It's so nice to meet you!"

I tried to disentangle myself. "Um, yes, hi." The hug was ongoing, and she was surprisingly tenacious. "I'm Dash. Nice to, uh, meet you."

After one final squeeze, she released me and stepped back. "You are going to *love* Hemlock House. Isn't it amazing? You're going to love it!" And then, just for good measure, she bounced on her toes and clapped her hands. "It's amazing!"

"So amazing," I said because I honestly had no idea what to say.

"I do all sorts of things for Vivienne," Millie said. "I bring her coffee. Oh! I work at Chipper. That's the coffee shop. And I bring her sandwiches sometimes, only she doesn't always like how they make the sandwiches, so then she writes down a HUGE LIST—" I'm using capital letters because at that point, Millie got very loud and also used her hands to show me how big the list was. "—of how she wants them to make it, and then I take them the list, and then they make the sandwich exactly how she wants it, and it is *so good*, like better than any sandwich I've ever had. Oh! And the sandwich place is called The Mermaid's Gill, only it was supposed to be Grill, but they didn't make the sign right, and then Fred didn't have to pay for it." She stopped for breath and added, "Or not all of it, I don't think. Oh! And—"

"Millie, I'm giving Dashiell a tour—"

"Just Dash," I put in.

Vivienne powered on. "—so you'll have to excuse us."

"Of course!" Millie hugged me again and darted toward the kitchen, shouting back, "It was so nice to meet you!"

I wondered, as the silence settled back down, if this was how people felt after they got picked up by a tornado.

"She's very…" Vivienne began doubtfully.

Then Millie's voice carried from the kitchen. "Oh my God, Indira, have you met Dash yet? He's so cute. So, so, so, cute! Oh my God, he's dreamy! I think I'm in love!"

"…enthusiastic," Vivienne finished.

"Oh!" That was Millie again. Apparently, solid-wood doors and inches of lath and plaster weren't up to the task of quieting her. "Unless he's gay! Oh my God, that would be even BETTER!"

(The capitalization doesn't fully convey the experience.)

"Uh," I said.

Vivienne made a tutting noise and pushed open the kitchen door. "Nothing to worry about, dear. Hastings Rock is very accepting."

"That's not what I was worried about—" I tried, but Vivienne had already pressed on without me, so I followed her into the kitchen.

"This is Indira," Vivienne said, gesturing to the woman with the witch-streak of white hair. "Indira, this is Dashiell."

"Actually, it's—"

"It's nice to meet you," Indira said over me. She had a lovely, low voice. "Do you have any dietary restrictions?"

"No."

"What about preferences? Things you won't eat?"

"Uh, no?"

She smiled. "Don't worry; we aren't too adventurous, and I'll let you know if I'm planning something I think you might not like. I keep snacks in the refrigerator, so please help yourself. I do ask, however, that you not use the kitchen to cook. As I explain to all of Vivienne's guests, this is my workspace, and I hope you'll respect it the same way I respect your personal space."

There didn't seem to be anything I could say to that except: "Of course."

"If you have any special requests," Vivienne said, "Indira will be happy to accommodate you."

"Another thing I explain to all of Vivienne's guests," Indira said in that same, hello-we're-friends-but-don't-screw-around voice, "is that, although I live on the property, I am not an on-call employee. I have contracted hours when I work for Vivienne. The rest of my time is my own, so if you have a midnight craving, I suggest helping yourself to snacks and leftovers, or you're always free to bike into town." Another polite, no-nonsense smile. "I promise I won't be offended if you choose to eat out, but I do like to know, if possible, so we can avoid food waste."

"Sure," I said—because again, what else was I going to say? "Of course." And then, because it felt like I had to say something, I asked, "Was that your son?"

The sudden silence was suffocating. Vivienne turned her head slowly toward Indira, and one eyebrow came up.

Indira's expression was flat and unreadable.

"I thought we talked about this," Vivienne said.

"We did," Indira said.

"I thought the issue was resolved."

"It is."

"Wonderful," Vivienne said the way people say it when they mean a word you can't print in the newspaper.

Indira tried to keep up her end of the staring match. Then she turned and chopped an onion in half. One strong, swift *schick* of the knife. It sounded like the last thing Marie Antoinette ever heard.

Maybe Vivienne saw something on my face because her expression relaxed, and she motioned for me to follow her. She said in a low voice, "I'm sorry. A bit of an ongoing disagreement. Indira can be a bit...stormy, but you wouldn't believe what she can do in a kitchen."

Build a gingerbread house to lure children in, I thought as I followed Vivienne through another door. Roast them at 425 for about an hour, and the meat falls right off the bone.

We passed through what must have been, in the olden days, the servants' dining room. It was still set up with a table and chairs, gingham curtains in the windows. They looked out on the sea cliffs. The boy I'd seen in the kitchen had come this way, but I didn't see him here. Vivienne pointed to a door and said, "That's the rear entrance. There's also a side entrance just around the stairs. The Blackwoods had strong opinions, like other wealthy people at the time, about servants not using the same spaces as decent people. The cellar's down there— I don't suppose you have a lot to store? We could make room."

"Not really," I said. "But thank you."

"Then I'll show you the billiards room and the den," she said, pushing through another door, which carried us back into the main hall. We had made a full loop of the ground floor, I realized, and Fox now lay on the tile directly ahead of us, snoring lightly. Vivienne chuffed a laugh as she indicated another pair of pocket doors.

Before I could open them, though, footsteps rang out in the vestibule, and a door closed a little too hard. Hasty steps moved toward us, and a moment later, a man entered the hall. He was white, with the comfortable padding of a man in middle-age, his receding hair clipped almost to the scalp. His suit looked like something out of a mortician's supply catalogue. He started for the stairs, glanced at Fox, and continued—obviously unfazed, which really said something.

"Mr. Huggins," Vivienne said, "perfect timing. This is Dashiell—"

"Dash is fine," I said.

"—and we've just about finished the tour. Why don't you get set up in my study, and we'll complete the necessary paperwork?" In an aside to me, Vivienne said with a smile, "Mr. Huggins is a fiend for forms."

Huggins stared at me, as though he weren't really seeing me. Little beads of sweat dotted his forehead, and he had an unhealthy cast to his complexion. "Vivienne, we need to talk."

Something changed in Vivienne's face—I wanted to call it surprise, but it wasn't quite that. Then it was gone. She squeezed my arm and said, "Dashiell, why don't you bring in your luggage and make yourself at home? I'm going to have a quick chat with Mr. Huggins."

"Oh, right. Sure. I, uh—I didn't know where to park, actually, so I left my car down on the road."

"Of course. Come right up the drive and follow it to the back. The coach house is technically the motor house, now, I suppose. You can let yourself in through the side and open the overhead door. We'll find you one of those remote thingies. Oh, please don't go poking around—Indira lives on the second floor, and she's protective of her space."

Why wouldn't she be, I thought. She's got all those children she's fattening up.

"That was your car?" Huggins asked, dabbing at his forehead with a handkerchief. He finally seemed to have realized I was there. "Parked on the shoulder?"

"The Jeep," I said.

"You'd better get down there. We've got an overzealous deputy on the local force, and he looked like he was about to have it towed away."

I looked at Vivienne with what I hoped was an apology, and then I ran.

CHAPTER 2

After I rescued the Jeep from an extremely obdurate sheriff's deputy (Deputy Mai, for anybody who wants to put him on their naughty list), I didn't see Vivienne or Mr. Huggins the rest of the day. I did as Vivienne suggested and moved the Jeep into the coach house (er, motor house). I caught another glimpse of the boy from the kitchen. He was watching me from the corner of the house, and as soon as I noticed him, he darted out of sight. And then I went inside and, well, did absolutely nothing. At all. For the rest of the day.

I mean, sure, I carried my luggage up to my room. I unpacked. I put my clothes in the dresser, hung some more in the closet, loaded my books onto the shelves (yes, they were built-ins, and yes, they were on either side of the fireplace). I took stock of the room and decided that, even though it wasn't how I'd been living (Hugo had loved anything and everything mid-century modern), I liked it. The dark blue of the damask wallpaper. The antique sconces. Even the canopy bed (a few exploratory bounces told me the mattress was excellent), which made me feel, a little bit, like I was living in a fairy tale. But believe it or not, you can only spend so much time bouncing on a bed before you start to feel like you need medication, so I explored the house.

I saw the billiards room (another specimen of Victoriana, almost perfectly preserved) and the den (a mouth-watering array of books, plus club chairs you could swim in and, yes, a full bar), and the reception room, which had only ever been used once, when Ulysses S. Grant came to visit. (I made that up.) I nosed around the other bedrooms upstairs, and they all looked like mine. I decided that maybe Mr. Nathaniel Blackwood had loved horse paintings a little too much. I thought maybe he should have invested in landscapes. Or portraits of anemic-looking white people wearing way too much whalebone. Or a safety inspector to check out his balcony.

Indira caught me going through a dresser in one of the unoccupied bedrooms.

"Sorry," I said, sliding the drawer shut as fast as I could. "Vivienne said I could look around."

On the other hand, Vivienne hadn't said, *Go through this place like a B&E guy*, but I figured there was some wiggle room in the invitation.

Indira still hadn't said anything, so I added, "Occupational hazard of being a writer." My face heated. "We're snoops at heart."

Her face remained frozen in that look of pure professionalism. "Dinner is ready. If you're not hungry now, you'll find it in the refrigerator, and you can warm it up yourself."

"Is Vivienne eating?"

"Vivienne keeps her own hours. If she comes to dinner, the food is ready. If she doesn't, I leave it in the refrigerator."

"Right. It's just—she's been in there a long time."

Indira didn't do anything dramatic like look at the dresser I'd just been rifling. She didn't say anything like, *This area is off limits.* She didn't even put her hands on her hips.

"I'm sorry if I got you in trouble earlier," I said. "I didn't know—I guess I still don't know what happened. But I'm sorry."

She said, "I'll be in the kitchen for another hour if you need anything."

"Thank you."

The only answer was the click of her steps moving away.

I spent an agonizing few minutes debating whether I should go down and eat dinner now, which seemed like the polite thing to do, or wait until she'd had time to clear out of the kitchen, which seemed like the safe thing to do. But the polite thing won out, as it usually did (my parents had engrained that in me pretty well, along with the snooping), and I made my way down to the kitchen. Indira redirected me to the dining room, where she brought me my food (a filet of sole cooked to perfection, a lemony-and-herby rice pilaf, and garlicky broccoli). It was all healthy, which normally was a deal breaker for me, but it also happened to be delicious, so I decided to be magnanimous and let it slide just this once. I decided, though, that when I wasn't quite so terrified of Indira, I'd ask her where the Victorians had kept the deep fryer.

It was a lonely meal. The house felt chilly, and even though it was June, the day had persisted in its grungy grayness, the marine layer thickening as it came off the water. Once, I thought I heard laughter from the servants' dining room, but the old house swallowed up sounds, and after a minute, I figured I was imagining things.

When I went upstairs, a strip of light still showed under Vivienne's door.

I spent the rest of the evening in my room, alternating between reading and watching cat videos on my phone. The thing about cat videos is that they're like popcorn (or, I suppose, perfectly braised children): once you eat one, you have to have more. In other words, I didn't get very far in my Lawrence Block novel. Part of that had to do with the fact that I was exhausted; Vivienne had been right about the rough start to the day, and I could barely keep my eyes open. I fell asleep watching a kitten try to climb out of an Instant Pot (why it was in there in the first place, I had no idea), and I woke sometime later to a loud noise. My brain decoded it as a door slamming. The clock by the bed (not the intimidatingly expensive one on the mantel, but a genuine Radio Shack with a red digital display) said it was just after midnight. A car started. My window looked out on the front of the house, and a moment later, I saw headlights moving down the drive. I fell asleep again almost immediately.

I wasn't a morning person. That was putting it, well, kindly. Imagine a Romero zombie shuffling around, moaning, "Brains," and you're on the right track. I'm a firm believer that nothing good happens before the sun is up, and nothing great happens before noon. But, since this was technically my first day on the job, I got up at the crack of dawn. Eight am. Okay, eight-thirty. Okay, I got out of bed at nine, but I was awake before that, promise. And then I promptly had no idea what to do aside from the usual morning emergency of finding a large amount of coffee as quickly as possible.

My bedroom had a Jack-and-Jill bathroom, which meant I shared it with the bedroom next to mine. I probably wouldn't have loved that layout if there had been anyone to share with, but since it was just me, it was fine—plus both doors locked, so I didn't have to worry about anyone wandering in on me. (Millie came to mind; I had a horrifying, and thankfully momentary, vision, of her ripping back the curtain, staring at me naked, and announcing, CUTE!) That thought helped me wake up. So did the fact that the house was, well, freezing.

Maybe it wasn't technically freezing, but it felt like it was. I mean, it was June. In Providence, we'd been getting into the 80s, with plenty of sun. Growing up in Portsmouth, the summer days had been warm and bright (and, let's face it, humid). But here, the day was overcast again, and everything I touched felt like ice. On top of that, the house had that persistent damp common to all oceanside towns. It wasn't new to me, and it wasn't necessarily unpleasant, but combined with the cold, it made me grateful Mr. Nathaniel Blackwood had believed strongly in fireplaces. I shivered as I dried myself off, and I kept waiting for my breath to mist in the air as I made a mad dash back to my room to get dressed. I found a pair of gray shorts, one of my favorite tees (it says *I Paused My Game To Be Here*), and white sneakers (Mexico 66, in case anyone cares). It was my first day, and I was going to look cute even if I died from exposure. I'd be a modern-day hero, probably. Another Shackleton.

When I emerged from my room, the door to Vivienne's study was closed. So was the door to her bedroom. I waited for a minute (okay, I crept over to her bedroom door, and then to the study) and listened. Nothing. Which was…great, right? I mean, if Vivienne wasn't a morning person, and I wasn't a morning person (although years of writing workshops had trained me to say, I'm not a morning person *yet*), then that would work out perfectly. Plus, she'd had a late night with Huggins. Whatever it was, it must have been serious to keep them locked up together for so long.

Although, if I were being honest, that door slamming in the middle of the night had hung on to me. Who slams a door in the middle of the night? Not a happy camper. Maybe Huggins was a morning person. Maybe he wanted to be in bed by eight, and he'd been feeling a little of what I was feeling right now. Which more or less could be summed up like this: if I didn't get some coffee soon, I wasn't responsible for my actions.

I made my way downstairs. I thought about trying the servants' dining room. But maybe that would be presumptuous; maybe I was supposed to use the, uh, proper dining room. Or should I just help myself in the kitchen. Too many possibilities; and then genius struck.

When I went outside, the day was even colder than I'd expected. The wind off the ocean cut through my T-shirt and shorts and raised goose bumps on my exposed skin. It ruffled my hair, which I was realizing now, I'd forgotten to comb. It was raining, but so lightly that it only misted my glasses. I thought about going back—I'd packed a jacket—but it was, technically, summer. So, I was going to dress like it was summer. The locals were probably all taking this in stride. Everybody was probably in swimsuits, soaking up sun (or at least cosmic radiation).

I got my car out of the coach/motor house and drove into town. That was the beauty of an intense desire to avoid all social interactions, especially potentially awkward ones: your brain came up with all sorts of creative solutions. Like, if you can't decide whether to go through door A or door B, instead, you literally run out of the house and drive away so that you never have to actually deal with your problems. That's called a life hack.

My drive took me through the lush growth of the Oregon Coast. Massive conifers turned the road into a tunnel, and fog hung in the branches. Ferns filled out the understory. Hills rose and fell, and where the ground dropped away, I looked down on misty ravines where more spruce and fir speared upward. Even with my window up, I could smell the slight hint of evergreen, of cedar, of rich, dark soil, and of course, the salt-tang of the sea. I drove with my headlights on because it was so gloomy; I only saw one other car, and it had its headlights on too.

It wasn't far to Hastings Rock; Hemlock House was still technically within the city limits. But it felt far. It felt, in fact, like I was driving through another world. (If I'm allowed to nerd out fully and completely for one tiny second, I felt like I was in a *Twilight* movie.) And when the trees thinned and I saw the first outbuildings of Hastings Rock appear—a Sinclair service station with halogen lights, a matchbox-sized shave ice stand in an empty gravel lot, a mobile home with firewood ricked along one side—something in my chest eased, and I thought maybe this was how astronauts felt.

The Maps app on my phone began working once I was clear of the trees, and I found the (apparently) one and only coffee shop in town. It wasn't a Starbucks. It wasn't a Dutch Bros. It wasn't a Stumptown (I'd heard great things about them). It wasn't even a Dunkin'. It was a place called Chipper, and I realized, with a name like that, I was in trouble.

It was a small building shoehorned onto a corner, with board-and-batten siding painted bright yellow. In the window, someone had chalked a smiling sun. A line of people ran out the door, men and women and children, all of them with the same Romero zombified look, which said we were all in the same boat. It shouldn't have surprised me; Hastings Rock was a tourist town, after all. From what I'd learned (from Google and Wikipedia, on crappy motel Wi-Fi, as I'd driven across the country), the town still had some industry, but every year, more and more of its revenue was tourism. And tourist season ran from June to September. I checked my phone just to make sure, but no other coffee shops showed up. Which was perfect. In a town of thousands, there was only one coffee shop. That made sense. That was great. Maybe I could drive around, find a grocery store or a gas station with coffee—but then, I liked good coffee, and I didn't have anything pressing—but then, what if Vivienne was already awake and working and she was wondering where I was and waiting for me—

Fortunately, the line moved—if not quickly, at least steadily. When we finally got inside, I saw that Chipper lived up to its name: the walls were that same bright yellow, with smiles and suns painted everywhere. As I watched, a little boy with a crayon was adding yet another smile. The shop had booths and seating clusters with driftwood accents, and well-tended ferns softened the space. Soft music played in the background—acoustic pop, probably on a playlist called "Coffee House Vibes" or something similar. A Black woman with her hair in beaded braids laughed as a white woman told a story with expansive hand gestures. The espresso machine shrieked as it released a cloud of steam. A girl who had to be ten, eyes glued to her tablet, walked into me from behind. She didn't even look up; her mom just steered her toward a booth and mouthed an apology. So yes, Chipper was small and crowded and noisy, none of which were my scene, but it was also undeniably cute. Or, as Millie would have put it, CUTE.

The coffee shop also had a perfect location on Main Street. It was a few blocks from the water, so you couldn't see the boardwalk or the ocean, but the display windows gave a great view of downtown Hastings Rock, which was, in a word, picturesque—an architectural jumble of timber frame and modern coastal and even a few well-preserved Victorian homes (which I guessed had been inspired by Hemlock House), with everything clean and well-maintained and tastefully commercial. The whole point, after all, was to get people to spend their money, whether it be at a taffy "workshop" (which sounded impressively artisanal) or an art "gallery" (which sounded impressively sophisticated) or

Seaside Sips Wine Tasting (which sounded impressively free of children). Vivienne had mentioned that Fox was an artist, and I wondered if they had a gallery or a studio or something nearby—

"DASH!"

I didn't even have to look around.

But, of course, I did.

Millie stood behind the counter, and it came back to me: she had mentioned, the day before, that she worked at Chipper. She'd even said that she brought Vivienne her coffee. Now, as the family ahead of me moved aside, I found myself stepping up to order, face to face with Millie. The same cloud of blond flyaways. The same sense of frenetic energy. Caffeinated energy, I realized. Like someone had hooked her up to an espresso IV.

"Oh my God, Dash, I was just telling Tessa about you. Tessa, this is DASH!"

Tessa was a weary-eyed woman with hair dye on her collar. She didn't react to Millie (no sign, for example, that Millie had just blown out her eardrum). She just gave me a smile and said, "You just moved into Hemlock House."

"Uh, yes."

For a moment, her smile got a little bigger. "Millie told us all about it. Hate to break it to you, but if Millie knows, everybody knows."

Millie nodded enthusiastically. "And he's so smart, and he's such a great writer, and Vivienne is obsessed with him, and he's going to be famous one day."

"I probably won't—" I tried.

"What do you want this morning, hon?" Tessa asked.

"The campfire latte," I said. "Can you do oat milk?" Oat milk sounded like a healthy, responsible adult thing to order. It didn't stop me from asking, "And double marshmallow sauce?"

"Write it down," Tessa told Millie, who seized a paper cup and a pen and began jotting furiously, breaking now and then to look up and beam at me.

"Anything else?" She eyed me, and even though she couldn't have been ten years older, added, "Something to eat?"

"The, uh, bagel sandwich. The everything one."

"Make sure it's toasted," Tessa said.

Millie was off like a shot. "Oh definitely, toasted is the best. Dash, one time I didn't toast mine, and I was like, YUCK because the texture wasn't right—"

She kept talking, in case you're wondering, but as she moved back to prepare the food, it was harder to hear her. Well, it wasn't, actually. That girl had an impressive set of lungs. But it seemed like far enough that I could pretend not to hear her.

Tessa settled up with me at the register and directed me to the pickup zone. I had about sixty seconds of peace before—

"DASH! Dash over here! Dash, can you hear me? I saw your eyebrow twitch."

People got caught in undertows and riptides every year. They got washed out to sea and drowned, and nobody could help them. They couldn't even help themselves; eventually, they wore themselves out struggling against the current, and they went under.

I drifted over to the espresso machine.

Millie's head didn't quite clear the machine, but that didn't stop her. "Do you have something wrong with your hearing? Sometimes my mom says her ears are tired. What are your parents like? Where are you from? Do you have any brothers or sisters? I have two brothers, and their names are Paul and Ryan, and two sisters, and their names are Kassandra and Angeline. Oh, and my mom and dad, of course. Duh! Their names are Matthew and Christine. Matthew and Christine Naught. Did you always want to meet Vivienne? Was that your life dream? I don't know what my life dream is, but Tessa says I don't need to know that yet, and it seems like so much pressure. Are you under a lot of pressure? I bet so. One time Vivienne was under so much pressure that her eye started twitching, and I asked her if there was anything I could do to help, and she *yelled* at me." She came around the machine and, with a flourish, presented me with the sandwich and the latte. "Double marshmallow sauce, just the way you like it. Do you have any pets? My dog's name was Chuck Norris, but he died a few years ago. Do you have a girlfriend? Is she beautiful? How old is she? Is she blond?"

And now, of course, was when she chose to stop talking. Apparently, so had everyone else because the coffee shop seemed remarkably quiet, even with so many people in it.

"No girlfriend," I said and tried for a smile. And then, as bait, "I do have a sister, though. Her name's Dorothy."

But Millie was not to be distracted. "What about a boyfriend? Or a partner? Or a throuple? Or—"

"Nope," I said. "Nobody." And then, since I had an idea which direction this was going, I tried to head it off. "I broke up with my boyfriend before I moved here."

"OH MY GOD!"

I kid you not, the glass rattled in the windows.

"Did he break your heart? Did he cheat on you? Was he a jerk? Should I beat him up? Tessa, I have to go get on a plane to beat someone up."

"Quad espresso, one pump cinnamon sauce, two-percent," Tessa called back.

The distress in Millie's face told me she had heard Tessa, but she wasn't quite ready to abandon this sinking ship of a conversation.

"I'd better run," I said. "Nice to meet you."

"We already met, remember? It was yesterday, and Indira told me to distract Vivienne because Keme was in the kitchen, and—" She was already coming around the counter, untying her apron, apparently having completely forgotten (or no longer caring) that she was working.

"Millie," Tessa called.

"I think she wants you to make that drink," I said.

"Oh dang. You know, we should totally hang out, like, I'm off work today at three, but then I have to go to my other job—"

"Yes," I said, creeping backwards, hoping that my natural instinct to flee every and all social encounters would guide me to the door. "Sure. Sounds great."

"Maybe I should get your number!"

My back bumped the door, a bell jingled, and I said a prayer that I wouldn't crush any children or trample any senior citizens as I shoved it open and darted outside.

The line, of course, was gone, which was my luck. And although the day had brightened some, the cloud layer meant it was still cool. I shivered; if anything, the day felt even colder after the warmth of the coffee shop. Then I noticed that people on the sidewalk were definitely not dressed in what I would consider summer wear. I saw a fair number of people in shorts, but just as many wore jeans or leggings. Almost everyone had a hoodie or a sweatshirt or a sweater or a thermal-knit long-sleeve. Layers, in other words. A few people even had coats. It was like that Mark Twain quote about San Francisco, I realized. So much for locals who were immune to the elements. I guess I'd be buying more layers. Lots and lots of layers. And, maybe, a can of bear spray for the next time Millie showed up.

I immediately felt bad about the thought. She was nice. Actually, she was lovely—authentic and kind and happy. This was a Dash problem, that was all. Too many people. Too much noise. And, of course, the...experience of talking to Millie, which was probably more talking than I'd done in the last year of my life. That had been the beauty of being an adjunct professor. I could teach my assigned classes, meet with the occasional student, and spend the rest of my time safely—and silently—buried in my office. Even at home, Hugo and I had always been comfortable with silence.

Then I spotted the ticket. It had been slipped under the windshield wiper. I stared at it for a moment in disbelief. And then I spotted the red curb. And the fire hydrant. I tossed the ticket into the Jeep with all the other papers and headed back to Hemlock House.

I followed the same two-lane out of Hastings Rock proper and into the dark tunnel of spruce and fir. I rolled down the windows and caught the sweet smell of resin and bark and duff. I tried not to think about the disastrous trip into town. In a few months, I'd probably be laughing about it. It would be a great story to tell, how I'd had a rocky start but now everything was wonderful. That kind of story. I could hear myself telling it: *And then I came out of Chipper, and there was a ticket on the Jeep!* It worked. After a few minutes, it all felt distant, better. I'd learned a long time ago that telling stories could make just about anything better.

When I got to Hemlock House, I went through the rigmarole of opening the coach house (I'd given up on motor house—it just didn't roll off the tongue) and parking inside. I hit the button to send the overhead door rattling down, and then I made my way to the house. Even up here on the sea cliffs, the sound of the surf breaking was enormous. Big combers were rolling in, and when the waves crashed against rock, the sound was enormous. Spray tinkled up, catching the light like aluminum flitter—

Something red bobbed in the water. I moved closer to the edge of the cliff. I forgot the coffee and the bagel. I couldn't hear the sound of the waves. I stared for what felt like a long time at that swatch of red. My brain kept telling me what it was, and I kept saying no. I remembered her red sweater. I kept thinking it couldn't be.

I didn't even remember putting down the coffee. I had my phone pressed to my ear, and a man answered, "911, what is your emergency?"

"I think—I think there's been an accident."

CHAPTER 3

Sheriff's deputies came. A man and woman in uniform, first. They got on the radio, and more came. Eventually, a woman whose name tag said Starks moved me into the kitchen. Indira was there with the same boy I'd seen yesterday. They both looked at me, and then the boy stared down at the floor between his feet. Bare feet, I noticed. And the same board shorts. The same tee that looked stiff with salt. Indira, though, kept her gaze on me. Finally, she asked, "Is it Vivienne?"

"I don't know. Maybe. It looked like her sweater."

I didn't want to think about what I'd seen. It had been bad enough seeing it once—thank God I'd been far enough that I couldn't make out the details. I tried to turn it into a story: coming home, parking in the garage, the pure chance of spotting something red. If it had been another color, I might not have even noticed. That helped for a while. But other thoughts started to creep in. Vivienne's story about the balcony. About Nathaniel Blackwood and his unnamed bride falling to their deaths. How I'd made a joke about staying off the balconies. I'd made a joke. I was sweating, I realized, my face hot and greasy. I thought I was going to be sick.

We were there for a long time. Men and women came and went. I could hear them going through the house. Raised voices. Questions. The words indistinguishable. A few passed through the kitchen, slowing to look at us, but nobody stopped. Nobody talked to us. Nobody was watching us. A part of me—

a part that was still in shock—had a dry little laugh. I decided we weren't suspects, at the very least, since any decent law enforcement officer would have known to separate the suspects.

A couple of hours passed before footsteps came from the servants' dining room and a man entered the kitchen. He was white, thin, with a long face and a pronounced jaw. His hair looked like somebody had airbrushed it onto his scalp. A gold badge pinned to his khaki uniform said SHERIFF. He looked at Indira and nodded.

Indira covered her eyes with one hand. The boy squeezed her free hand, and Indira gripped him back.

"It's her?" I asked. "It's Vivienne?"

The sheriff turned his attention on me. After a long moment, he said, "You're Mr. Dane, is that correct? Dashiell Dane?"

"Yes. Is it Vivienne?"

"Mr. Dane, do you have identification?"

"Yes, I—what?"

"Let's start with your ID."

I took my driver's license from my wallet and handed it to him. He studied it for a minute, and then he called, "Bobby?" A deputy stepped into the room, and I recognized him immediately: golden skin, glossy black hair in a razor part, and a way of carrying himself that made me forget, for a moment, that he was a few inches shorter than me (although in way better shape). This was the deputy who had ticketed me on my first day for leaving the Wrangler parked on the side of the road. And I had a sneaking suspicion he'd given me my second ticket as well. The sheriff handed him my license, and he left without a word. Then the sheriff looked at me again, longer this time, the silence stretching until it felt like it would snap.

"Indira," he said, still looking at me. "You go on back to your place. Keme, can't you be a normal kid for once?"

The boy—Keme—shot the sheriff an unreadable look, but he rose from his chair without a word and padded toward the door. Indira went with him, her eyes red as she wiped tears from her cheeks.

"Mr. Dane," the sheriff said, "my name is Sheriff Jakes. I'm sorry this is how we had to meet. I've got a few questions that I hope you can help me with."

"Of course."

"Did I get it right that you came here yesterday?"

I nodded.

"And you're staying at Hemlock House?"

"I'm living here. I moved here."

"Really? What were you doing before?"

"Teaching. Just an adjunct position."

"That sounds nice," the sheriff said. He reached up like he might touch that airbrushed-on hair, but he lowered his hand before he could. "We can't get enough teachers. So, what brings you to Hastings Rock?"

"A job. I'm Vivienne's administrative assistant."

The sheriff nodded, but he said, "That's quite a change, isn't it? You've got a Rhode Island license, and you moved all the way across the country, left your family and friends behind, to start a job as a secretary."

"Well, administrative assistants—"

"Why don't you explain that to me?"

For a moment, all I could do was stare at him. "I'm a writer. A mystery writer. And Vivienne is one of the most famous authors in the world." The sheriff didn't respond, so I added, "I jumped at the opportunity."

He made a noise that could have meant anything. "What's the nature of your relationship with Ms. Carver?"

"I just told you—she's my boss, I guess. What's going on? Was that her? Why won't you tell me what happened?"

The sheriff pulled out a straight-backed chair and sat. "Mr. Dane, Vivienne Carver died sometime last night from a fall. Now, I don't know you, and you're new to this house, and I'd like you tell me the nature of your relationship with Ms. Carver."

"Oh my God, she's dead? That was really her?" I rubbed my face. "We didn't have a relationship. She knows my parents—knew my parents. I'd never met her before." I couldn't seem to get any words out. "She was so kind."

"Why don't we go over your movements from the last twenty-four hours?"

That cut through the fog. I raised my head. "Excuse me?"

"Where have you been. What have you been doing. That kind of thing."

The mystery writer in me long-jumped to the worst possible situation: "Am I a suspect? Wait, do I need a lawyer?"

"Right now, Mr. Dane, you're someone who's not answering some simple questions. I'd like to finish this conversation so I can move on with my investigation. You're not under arrest, if that's what you're asking. So, if you want to call a lawyer, go right ahead."

I thought about it. But it seemed...excessive. And even though I'd written plenty of stories about people demanding an attorney, now that I found myself in the same situation, there was an unexpected pressure not to make a scene. Not to do anything, in fact, that might make me look guilty. Which was a bizarre thought, but I couldn't help it. "I—I got to Hemlock House yesterday morning around nine. I stayed in a motel outside Portland, and I drove the rest of the way in the morning. I met with Ms. Carver, we agreed I'd start the job, and then she wanted me to talk to her attorney, Mr. Higgins."

"Huggins," the sheriff said.

"Right, Mr. Huggins. They were in her office all day. Literally all day. I got settled in my room. Unpacked, that kind of thing. I didn't have anything else to do. I ate dinner here. I read. I fell asleep—oh! Someone slammed a door. And there was a car." I related, as best I could, how I'd been woken, and what I'd seen. If my powers of recollection impressed the sheriff, he didn't show it. "This morning, I went into town for coffee." I gestured miserably to the bagel and coffee, now cold, on the kitchen counter. "That's all."

"Can anyone verify your movements?"

Now that sounded like a question that called for a lawyer, but there was something about the sheriff's impersonal, hard gaze that made me say, "I've got receipts. From the motel. And Indira was here. And someone named Fox. And Millie. Mr. Huggins, too, I guess. And then this morning, I saw Millie again when I got coffee."

"What about last night?"

"I was in my room."

"Can anyone corroborate that?"

I opened my mouth, but I knew the sheriff already knew the answer: no. Nobody had been in the house except for me and Vivienne. The best I could come up with was a shake of my head.

"Tell me, Mr. Dane, have you ever been inside Ms. Carver's bedroom?"

"No."

"Never?"

"No!"

"Are you in possession of any of Ms. Carver's belongings?"

"What in the world—of course not!"

"When was the last time you saw or spoke to Ms. Carver?"

"In the hall, when Mr. Huggins arrived."

"Are you aware of any disputes, legal troubles, or personal conflicts in Ms. Carver's life?"

"No."

"Did Ms. Carver express concerns about her safety?"

I almost told him about that strange story about Nathaniel Blackwood and his wife. Somehow, I managed to stop myself, and I shook my head.

"Was Ms. Carver involved in any significant financial transactions recently? Or changes in her financial state?"

"Are you kidding? I talked to her one time."

"What about you, Mr. Dane? Have you had any major changes recently in your personal or professional life?"

"I just told you I have."

"Emotional or financial difficulties?"

I stared at him. I'd grown up with parents who specialized in the macabre, where talking and reading and thinking about things like exotic murders and due process and, yes, homicide interviews were part of daily life. And I knew, now, my gut had been right. The sheriff could say whatever he wanted, but I knew I was a suspect. And the only smart thing to do was to stop talking.

Instead, though, I ran my mouth. "Why are you sitting here talking to me? I already told you everything. I barely knew her. I'm sorry for what happened to her, but it's not like we were close. Shouldn't you be out there, documenting the scene or waiting for the coroner or medical examiner or whoever it is, protecting the scene from the elements so you can process it, canvassing for witnesses? Shouldn't you be doing literally anything else except sitting here talking to me?"

The sheriff pursed his lips. "Believe it or not, Mr. Dane, I know how to do my job. As sheriff, I'm an authorized medical-legal investigator for the State of Oregon. We're not waiting for the district medical examiner because I've already ordered the body removed from the scene. My deputies know how to document evidence. The scene of the crime, as far as I'm concerned, is inside this house. And this is an isolated stretch of coast on the outskirts of a small town. If you've got witnesses, I'd love to meet them."

The scene of the crime is inside this house. I shook my head and stood. "I'm done with this conversation."

"Mr. Dane, don't be difficult. I've only got a few more questions."

"You can set up a meeting with my lawyer."

"You didn't leave your room? Not once last night?"

I knew better than to answer, but I said, "No, I never left my room. And no, I don't have an alibi, I don't have any witnesses, I don't have anyone who can corroborate my statement, so I guess you'll just have to take my word for it."

He nodded. And then he said, "I'd like to show you something, and you can decide if you'd like to talk some more."

Without waiting for a response, he stood and headed out of the kitchen. I followed him through the servants' dining room, up the back set of stairs, and emerged into the upstairs hall. A deputy was photographing Vivienne's door. Maybe the sheriff saw the question on my face because he said, "Her bedroom door was still locked. The door to her study, too. We had to force one of the doors to get in. So, that's one of the questions, isn't it? How did someone get inside Vivienne's room last night?"

A part of my brain noticed his switch from Ms. Carver to Vivienne. That same part of me noticed the edge in his voice. The barely hidden anger.

"Maybe it was an accident," I said. My brain kept telling me to stop talking, but I couldn't seem to hit the brakes. "Maybe it was suicide."

The sheriff didn't respond.

"If that's what you wanted to show me," I said, "then you're out of luck, because I didn't even know those doors were locked, and I don't have any idea how—"

"That's not what I wanted to show you."

The sheriff stopped at my door and pushed it open. I was surprised, and then not, to see Deputy Bobby going through the dresser, lifting out my clothes with gloved hands and examining each article. He looked up, and something like chagrin passed over his face when he saw me, but then the emotion was gone.

Two words popped into my head: search warrant. I opened my mouth, about to scream *lawsuit*, but before I could, I saw what the sheriff had wanted to show me.

The back of my big old fireplace stood at a ninety-degree angle, like it had pivoted on a hidden axis. And through the opening it had created, I could see another bedroom: a large canopy bed, an antique dresser, and deputies going over every inch of the space for evidence.

A secret door, my brain said. Twelve-year-old me would have been thrilled to live in a house with a secret door. But I knew what this meant. I knew why the sheriff had kept asking if I'd left my room the night before. I knew why he'd wanted to show me this. Because no one could have gotten into Vivienne's room; the doors had been locked. No one except me, with the secret passage in my bedroom. And because I hadn't known that, I'd sat there and hammered the final nails into my own coffin.

CHAPTER 4

The sheriff didn't arrest me, which seems like a miracle, but he did have Deputy Bobby take me to the station. I sat in an interview room, alone, for a long time. And then, for an even longer time, I sat there while the sheriff asked me questions. I didn't say anything. I wish I could say that a lifetime of hearing my parents argue about police procedures had prepared me for this, and that I was smart enough and savvy enough to remain silent until they either arrested me or let me go. But the truth is I was in shock.

The sheriff and his deputies believed someone had killed Vivienne. And they believed that someone had been me.

Eventually, I left. The sheriff didn't like it. He shouted. He threatened. He told me I was making a huge mistake. But by then, I'd recovered enough to remember my rights. He didn't arrest me, so I left.

Of course, I only made it as far as the parking lot before I realized I had no car, no friends, and nowhere to go. It was evening, and the gloomy day had settled into dark. Cold, damp dark. For a moment, the need to cry rolled over me, and I sucked in lungfuls of air that smelled like fish and motor oil and old cigarette smoke. Then I took out my phone to call an Uber.

No Ubers. Of course not.

"You all right?" The voice came from behind me, and when I turned around, Deputy Bobby was standing there in his civvies: an Aran sweater, jeans, boots that toed the line of trying a little too hard to be butch.

"Fine," I said.

He stared at me for what felt like an uncomfortably long time. Then he said, "Let me give you a ride home."

I almost said, *I don't have a home*. But that sounded maudlin even to me, and for lack of a better option, I let him lead me across the parking lot. He drove a Honda Pilot (black), which went with the boots. He followed me around to the passenger side and held the door for me.

"All that training," I said as I got into the seat. "Making sure the arrestee doesn't hit their head when they get in the car."

"You're not under arrest."

He shut the door gently and came around the SUV. We eased out of the lot, gravel crunching under the tires. He had music playing, something metal, but the volume turned low. I didn't recognize it; I wouldn't know [blank] from [blank] (fill in your metal bands of choice). I tried to remember the last time anyone had held the door for me.

We drove in silence. The dark thickened against the glass. Trees, stars, the gloss of headlights on wet pavement. Then I realized where we were going.

"I can't go back to Hemlock House."

"Okay. Where would you like to go?"

"I don't know. A motel. I can't get my stuff, can I?"

"Not yet; they haven't released the scene."

"Anywhere, then. It doesn't matter."

He turned the music off. "This is peak tourist season. You're not going to find a motel."

I shook my head and dropped back against the seat.

"Why can't you stay at Hemlock House?" Deputy Bobby asked.

"I don't know. Maybe because I'm a murder suspect?"

It took me a moment to recognize his silence as amusement. "You're kind of a smart aleck."

"I'm sorry. Being accused of killing an innocent woman brings out the snippiness."

For some reason, that made him smile. Not at me, but out at the darkness. It was a surprisingly goofy smile for someone who handed out tickets like they were candy and looked like he was in training to be an action figure. The sweater wasn't exactly form fitting, but I'd seen him in uniform, and Deputy Bobby was, well, jacked.

The smile faded, though, and he said, "Did you kill her?"

It was a strangely open question—no expectations weighted behind it, no hostility.

"No."

"Okay then."

He didn't exactly say, *What's the problem?*

I answered the question anyway. "But everybody thinks I did."

"But you didn't."

"But they think I did."

"But you didn't."

"Is this from Abbott and Costello? Did I lose a page of the script?"

"This is what I meant about being a smart aleck."

I was surprised to catch a smile on my face—a tired one, yes, but one that felt weirdly genuine. Before I could stop myself, I asked, "Why are you driving me home?"

"You needed a ride."

Well, I thought, if that wasn't the most confusing answer of all time, I didn't know what was.

"What are you going to do now?" he asked.

An unhappy laugh spilled out of me.

Deputy Bobby cocked an eyebrow.

"That's funny because one thing I'm good at in life is not making decisions. About anything. Ever. That's vintage Dash. I couldn't decide where to go to college. Then I couldn't decide what to study. Then I couldn't decide what kind of job I wanted. I write mysteries, in theory, and I can't decide who the killer is going to be. Heck, I can't even decide on an opening sentence."

"It was a dark and stormy night. That one always works."

"There's only room in this car for one smart aleck, thank you."

There was that grin again: boyish, almost silly. "You should stay at Hemlock House. There: that's one decision you don't have to make."

I made a face.

"Sorry," he said with a laugh. "It's already decided. No rethinking, considering, debating, or changing."

I took off my glasses and rubbed my eyes. That need to cry washed over me again, and my face prickled. Finally, I managed a thick, "Thanks."

"Things are going to work out," Deputy Bobby said as we pulled into the drive at Hemlock House. "The sheriff will keep investigating. I know it looks bad now, but you'll feel better in the morning."

"I'll feel better when I'm not the number one suspect," I said. "Who knows? Maybe there's someone even sketchier than me in Hastings Rock."

We finished the drive in silence; maybe I'd said something too stupid for words, or maybe Deputy Bobby didn't want to contradict me. It did seem like a long shot—I didn't think anyone else had a bedroom with a secret door that made it possible for them to commit an otherwise impossible murder.

Hemlock House rose on the cliffs ahead of us, painted by dramatic landscape lighting so that it looked like something out of a movie (horror or thriller, obviously). An imposing arched doorway, multi-paned windows, so many dang chimneys. It looked like Mr. Nathaniel Blackwood had started with a symmetrical design, maybe Georgian, and then a fit of Victorian madness had taken over—hence the turrets, towers, and, apparently, secret doors. It also looked distinctly creepy, if anyone wanted my opinion. And the fact that someone had managed to murder Vivienne inside her locked bedroom without waking me—or, for that matter, being noticed by anyone else—made me reconsider Deputy Bobby's suggestion I should stay here tonight alone.

If it even was murder, I told myself. If it wasn't an accident or suicide. Like Nathaniel Blackwood, I thought, and a crazy laugh tried to escape me. Like his bride.

When Deputy Bobby stopped in front of the house, he nodded at the cruisers parked on the drive and said, "You'll have company all night, I think. In case you were worried."

"Would you believe me if I said that doesn't really make me feel better?"

"Get some rest."

I opened the door and slid out of my seat. "Thanks for the ride, Deputy Bobby."

"That makes it sound like I'm on a kids' TV show."

I gave him a jaunty little salute, and I got the goofy smile in return.

"Goodnight, Mr. Dane."

"Just Dash," I said. I hesitated and added, "It was really kind of you." He didn't say anything, but for the first time, I noticed his eyes. They were a rich, earthy bronze I'd never seen on anyone. And there was something in them I didn't know how to read. I cleared my throat. "And that's being generous on my part since I suspect the whole point of this ride was to trick me into a confession somehow."

His hesitation surprised me, and for an instant, I thought he was going to say something. No, that wasn't quite right. I thought he was going to ask something. And then the moment passed, and the certainty came back into his face. His tone was slightly different, although I couldn't put my finger on how, when he said, "Goodnight, Dash."

I watched Deputy Bobby drive off, and then I went inside. The house was cold and damp and dark, and since I had no idea where the light switches were, I padded through the vestibule and into the hall in the gloom. Sounds drifted down the stairwell: voices, movement, too indistinct to make out anything useful. The deputies, I assumed, still processing the scene of the crime. Which, according to the warrant the sheriff had shown me, included my bedroom.

In the darkness of the hall, I stood and listened and thought I should just go home. I could get in the Jeep, spend the night in Portland, and be well on my way back to—where? My parents? I wanted to laugh. They'd love that. And then they'd go back to their books and their awards and their lives, and I'd turn into Emily Dickinson, shuttered in the attic until they brought me out for parties. Worse, actually. I'd be a ghost. The ghost of Dash who might have been. No, I couldn't go back to my parents.

And I couldn't run away either. Running away from my problems was how I'd gotten here in the first place. (Although, for the record, I still fully endorse running away as an all-purpose solution for avoiding things you don't want to deal with.) Maybe it was the fear, maybe it was the lingering shock, maybe it was simply logic—whatever it was, a part of me understood that I couldn't run away from this. Because running away would make me look guilty, and Sheriff Jakes already had me in his crosshairs. Deputy Bobby might believe that the investigation would continue, and I could hope and pray someone would show up at the sheriff's station and confess to Vivienne's murder. But the reality was that, as far as the sheriff and most of the town was concerned, the case was already solved: I had murdered Vivienne, and now they were just gathering evidence until they were ready to arrest me.

So, if someone was going to find Vivienne's killer, it would have to be me.

The thought was surprisingly bracing: a cool, clear relief from my normal indecision and the generalized anxiety that accompanied it. Even though the day had been long and exhausting and, quite frankly, horrible, I felt awake. Alert. Energized, even. I knew a lot about crime. I knew even more, specifically, about murder. I knew about police procedure, evidence, building a case. (I mean, I knew how to build a case in a mystery. In theory.) This stuff was my bread and butter; this was what my family lived for. (And that was a little red flag to bring up with my therapist.) But I could do this. I could. I would. I had to.

And the first place to start in any murder investigation was with the victim.

CHAPTER 5

I went up the grand staircase and took a look down the hall. The door to Vivienne's bedroom was open, as was the door to my room. In both rooms, the lights were on, and the sounds of movement came from each. A man called out, "Lauren, did you get more powder?"

"I told you to get it yourself." That was a woman. "Your legs aren't broken, are they?"

The man said a few choice words about what he (in a charming flash of misogyny) called "Women's libbers."

I ducked back into the stairwell and hurried down. If I'd been Will Gower, private investigator, I would have lucked out—the deputies would have been taking a smoke break, or they would have already finished processing the rooms, and one of them would be dozing lazily. But then, if I'd been Will Gower, my heart wouldn't have been beating as fast as a hummingbird's, and I wouldn't feel like I was about to enter the Guinness Book of World Records for being the first person to pass out and throw up at the same time.

When I reached the hall, I turned left and stepped into the servants' dining room. The room was brightly lit, and I realized I'd walked in on a group of people. Four people. Indira, the boy called Keme, Fox, and—

"DASH!"

I checked my ears for blood, which was a mistake because it gave Millie enough time to get free of her chair and crash into me with a hug.

"Let him go," Indira said. "Mr. Dane, are you all right? I wasn't sure I'd see you again."

I nodded. "I'm sorry I interrupted you."

"Not at all." The gap in the words was slight, but it was there. "Are you planning on staying at Hemlock House? I don't mean to be rude, but I would have thought—"

"We thought you were going to be in prison," Millie announced.

Fox choked on their coffee.

"I was going to say," Indira said with a look for Millie that Millie seemed oblivious to, "I would have thought you'd like to stay somewhere else."

"One of the deputies suggested I stay here." It wasn't exactly a lie. In fact, Deputy Bobby had pretty much decided for me. "Is that a problem?"

Indira shook her head slowly. "I assume that eventually, there will be considerations about the estate, but—no, Mr. Dane, that's not a problem."

"Dash, please."

"Would you like something to eat? Leftovers are in the fridge, or you're welcome to cake and coffee." She gestured at the spread in front of them—not only a beautifully iced layer cake, but chocolate chip cookies, a blueberry pie, and, for some reason, bacon. "I thought we could all use something sweet. The bacon is for Fox."

"I'm a slut for bacon," Fox said as though that explained everything.

"Actually—" My automatic reflex to flee any kind of social situation kicked in, the excuses piling up: I have a headache, I have to get some work done, I have to wash my hair. But I didn't. Maybe it was the fact that I wasn't thinking clearly after a long, horrible, confusing day. Maybe it was because I was tired and hungry and weak. Maybe it was simply because I was lonely. Instead, different words popped out of my mouth: "I'd love to."

I took a seat at the table. The servants' dining room was a good size, and even with five of us, it didn't feel cramped. It was homey, with a little cross-stitch sampler of what I thought might be huckleberries, a ceramic vase of little white roses on the table, and hooks near the door where several rain slickers hung. Even though it was quite possibly the only room in the house without a fireplace, it was snugly warm with what I guessed was the residual heat from Indira's baking. And it felt cozy, too. The vibe, for lack of a better word, of these people was good. They seemed to like each other. No, that wasn't quite right. They seemed like friends, even though they all seemed so different: Millie had to be twenty years younger than Indira and Fox, and Keme was at least a couple of years younger than her. But as soon as the word popped into my head, I knew it was right. They were friends. You could see it in the way Indira and Fox had taken Millie in stride, or the way Indira and Fox had talked about bacon, even the way Keme seemed to be a part of it, although the boy sat slightly back, removed from their circle.

"I didn't realize you all knew each other," I said as Indira loaded a plate with cake and then served coffee from a carafe. "How did you become friends?"

"Hastings Rock is a small town," Indira said with another of those neutral smiles. "If you'd like to take your food to one of the bedrooms, I can help you get set up for the night."

"Don't kick him out," Fox said. "He's interesting and new, and we're all so boring."

"And he's my best friend," Millie proclaimed. "We're all best friends, Dash. That includes you, too."

Keme made a face about that, and for some reason, it made Indira laugh.

"We're friends because we're the Last Picks," Fox said. I could hear how they said the words, the capital letters attached to them. "Like Indira said, Hastings Rock is a small town."

"Plus we love each other," Millie said.

Fox rolled their eyes. "That too."

"The Last Picks?" I asked.

Fox grinned. "You know, like the last picks in gym."

"Or for prom," Indira said drily.

"Or for your final presentation," Millie said, "and it's a group project, and someone even picks Robby Greaves before they pick you, even though Robby is suspended because he drew a—" She paused, her cheeks flooding with red. "—thing on the floor of the boy's locker room with a marker, and the group project is a PRESENTATION!"

I couldn't help it; a laugh escaped me. Fox's grin swept over their face again. Even Indira smiled, although it looked reluctant. Only Keme didn't. The boy's dark eyes were fastened on me, and his face was unreadable.

"I definitely qualify as a member," I said. "I've been a last pick pretty much my whole life."

"Nope," Millie said. "I don't believe it."

"I believe it," Fox said, and that made us all laugh again.

"I'm serious," I said. "For example, at the faculty party in the spring, we were supposed to play a trivia game. I didn't even qualify as a last pick—when they made the teams, nobody picked me. I mean nobody, not even when I was the last person. Finally, the department chair said she wouldn't play either so that the teams would be balanced."

At the time, it had been humiliating. Hugo had been furious when I'd told him. (In hindsight, I realize Hugo was probably furious for other reasons.) Fox burst out laughing, though, as did Millie, and even Indira gave a surprisingly genuine grin. Only Keme didn't, and now his expression wasn't unreadable. It was downright hostile.

The clarity of that dislike brought reality back: these people were being kind to me, but they—like Sheriff Jakes and the rest of the town—must have considered me the prime suspect for Vivienne's murder. And I hadn't come in here to eat cake and—I'd almost said *make friends*, but it had been so long since

I'd made a friend that I wasn't sure I knew how. Anyway, I had a mission, and, I now realized, this was a golden opportunity.

"You must have been close with Vivienne," I said. "I can't imagine how hard this is."

Keme was still trying to murder me with nothing but his eyes, but Indira's face became strangely composed—that professional façade I'd seen before, which I now realized covered a much more complicated woman. Fox, though, just snorted. And Millie, who clearly couldn't tell a lie to save her life, grimaced and stared down at the floor.

"Did I say something wrong?" I asked.

"No," Fox said.

"Not at all." Indira folded her napkin. "Vivienne's death is a tragedy."

Which didn't sound, I thought, like they'd been very close with her. Or that this was a particularly difficult situation for them. Indira made it sound like a tragedy in general. The way every murder was a tragedy.

"She was so kind to me," I said, "offering me this job, making sure I felt comfortable in the house. And, I mean, she was such a force, you know? Culturally, I mean. For decades."

Indira settled her newly folded napkin under her fork. Fox gazed off into the middle distance and played with one button of their vest.

"She gave me a job when nobody else would," Millie said. "Delivering her coffee."

"I can't stop thinking about what the sheriff asked me," I said. "He wanted to know if she'd had any personal conflicts, disputes, that kind of thing lately."

No one said anything for what felt like a long time. Then Fox shrugged.

"Or if she'd felt concerned for her safety," I said.

Keme stood so abruptly that his chair legs squeaked across the floor. He stormed to the door and disappeared into the darkness beyond, and the door crashed shut behind him.

"I'm sorry," Indira said. "Vivienne wasn't terribly kind to him, and I think he's still a bit upset that you said something to her. Not that you knew—I explained it to him."

I started to reply to that, but Fox was staring at me. Their mouth opened, and then, in a tone of disbelief, they said, "Are you interrogating us?"

"No!" But a full-body flush ran through me, stinging like pins and needles, and a distant part of me observed that Millie might not be the only one who couldn't lie. "I—"

Fox erupted in laughter. Millie started laughing too. They laughed so hard that they leaned against each other for support. Indira gave them a dirty look, but I could tell she was trying not to smile.

When they had finally recovered, I said, "I'm sorry."

"Oh God, don't be," Fox said. "Being suspected of murder is the first interesting thing that's happened to me in twenty years."

"Stop being so dramatic," Indira said.

"We only laughed," Millie said, "because we were going to try to interrogate you."

"You're not supposed to tell him!" Fox shouted, but they sounded amused more than angry. "Now I'm never going to weasel out all his secrets."

"None of us killed Vivienne," Indira said. She glanced at the door and added, "Keme spent the night at my place last night, and neither of us left."

Maybe Fox saw something on my face because they said in an undertone, "It's not like that. Keme just can't go home some nights; it's not safe." In a stronger voice, they added, "And I'm completely exonerated because I had a romantical guest."

"Oh my God," Millie said. "Not the lumberjack."

"Don't worry about my business."

"Fox, he's the worst."

"If you don't have anything nice to say, then don't say anything at all."

The expression on Indira's face told me she agreed with Millie, but she didn't say anything.

"Well, I was home all night," Millie said. "And I share a room with my sisters."

"There you go," Indira said, a little edge to her voice. "Does that satisfy you?"

"I'm sorry," I said. "I didn't mean—"

"She's upset because Keme's upset, and Keme's upset because—"

"Fox," Indira said.

Fox wrinkled their nose, but they stopped what they'd been about to say. "You want to figure out who really killed Vivienne so that you're off the hook. Yeah, we get it."

"Uh," I said, "not to sound rude, but you don't think I killed her?"

"Oh God no," Millie said. "You almost fainted when you had to decide what milk you wanted in your coffee."

"Hey!" The reaction slipped out of me before I could stop it, and I was surprised to see Millie—and Fox—grinning.

"You clearly didn't kill her," Indira said. "I saw you after you called the sheriff."

"I'm a little more skeptical, since you did have the amazing secret passage in your bedroom," Fox said, "but I'd still say I'm ninety percent certain you didn't kill her. You don't have the chutzpah."

"Thank you, I guess?"

"OH MY GOD!" Millie sat up, beaming again. "We can investigate together!"

"Oh no—" I tried.

"Finally," Fox said, cracking their knuckles. "I knew I didn't watch all twenty seasons of *Law & Order* for nothing."

"I really don't think—"

"This is a terrible idea," Indira said.

"Yes, exactly—"

"But I don't think we have any other option."

"Well, see, I work best alone—"

"No," Fox said, "you don't."

"You clearly need help, dear," Indira said. "And you haven't touched your cake."

Will Gower was a lone wolf. The man always on the outside looking in. He worked on his own to solve cases entire teams of police officers couldn't unravel. That was part of what made him so compelling: the white knight who walked the darkness alone, his grit and resolve carrying him to the successful conclusion of each mystery. But, I thought, maybe, every once in a while, Will Gower needed help. Every once in a while, he was allowed to phone a friend. Or maybe he wasn't a loner—maybe he had a partner? His girl—or boy—or agender person—Friday? Or maybe a bunch of Fridays, and one of them had a tendency to shout directly in your ear. So, I was both surprised and not surprised at the next words out of my mouth.

"We need to get into Vivienne's office."

Chapter 6

Indira, Millie, Fox, and I crouched at the end of the hall, watching. In Vivienne's bedroom (and mine), the deputies were busy carrying out their search.

"I still don't think this is a good idea," Indira whispered.

"Exactly." Millie did not whisper. Millie's volume could be generously described as conversational. Fox put a finger over their lips, and Millie grimaced and continued in a lower voice, "This is why I should be the one—"

"We're not getting into that argument again," I said.

"I don't know how you think I'm going to keep them occupied." Indira looked at the carafe of coffee in one hand and then at the basket in the other. "It takes five seconds to ask someone if they want a snack."

"But you brought all the snacks, right? And you're going to tell them about each snack. About dietary restrictions. About flavor profiles. About anything and everything. Because you're a brilliant chef, and that's going to be easy for you."

For a moment, before the cool mask fell into place again, Indira looked strangely gratified.

"Plus," Fox said, "you'll have Millie."

"Exactly!" It was still not, by any stretch of the imagination, a whisper.

"Give us two minutes," Fox said. "And then go."

"Wait, maybe you should do a sign so we know you're in position," Millie said. "You should crow. Like a crow. No, wait, that'd be too obvious. What sound does a fox make?"

Indira didn't actually clap a hand over Millie's mouth, but whatever she said, it worked nearly as well. Millie fell silent as Fox led me into one of the unoccupied bedrooms at the rear of the house. It didn't look too different from mine; the major difference was that the horse in this painting was brown instead of white, and instead of an imposing mantel clock, it had an equally imposing vase with silk flowers. Fox crossed to the Jack-and-Jill bathroom, which connected to another bedroom along the rear of the house, and from there, they opened the next door onto a stub of a hallway that intersected with the main hall. The door to Vivienne's study was almost directly opposite us. Another door opened off to the right, and an unadorned staircase ran up toward what I presumed was the attic.

Almost as soon as we were in position, Millie's voice floated down the hall: "But I want to ask them! Let me ask them!" Indira said something, and Millie said, "Then I get to ask them about the coffee."

"She's really getting into character," I whispered.

Fox rolled their eyes. That was my first clue that this was not, perhaps, part of the script.

Millie and Indira's voices grew louder as they came down the hall, and a moment later, the male deputy poked his head out of Vivienne's bedroom. He was a stocky white man with ruddled cheeks, hair buzzed to a zero. He radiated enough toxic masculinity to set off a Geiger counter.

"Excuse me," he said. "You can't be up here."

"I'm sorry, Dairek," Indira said. "I thought maybe—"

"Do you want any coffee?" Millie asked. "And Indira brought snacks."

"This is a crime scene," the female deputy said. She emerged a moment later: white with her brown hair in barrel curls, she had a way of standing like she thought she might be wearing heels. "We can't eat in here. We'd get crumbs everywhere."

"We can have coffee," Deputy Dairek said. He sounded like a man who had been forced to explain a lot of obvious things to the female half of the species over the years, things that were completely obvious to any healthy, straight, cis man. For example, why they should all want to date him. "We're not going to spill any coffee. And we can eat out in the hall."

"We're really not supposed to," the female deputy said to Indira.

Indira's smile was surprisingly warm. "I don't think Sheriff Jakes expects you to work all night without eating anything."

Indecision fluttered in the female deputy's face. Then she said, "It's got to be out in the hall."

"Let me set everything on this credenza," Indira said as she moved down the hall. The deputies followed her, passing our little side corridor where Fox and I still hid inside the bedroom. As the voices moved away, Fox eased the door open and slipped out into the hall. I followed a moment later. We crossed to the study door. With every step, I waited for one of the old boards to creak underfoot. But we made it in silence, and when Fox tried the door, it opened easily.

I blinked and whispered, "Are you wearing gloves?"

Fox grinned and produced a second pair from inside their vest. "I thought you were a mystery writer."

"That's more in theory than in practice."

"Time for the rubber to meet the road, then."

"And these," Indira was saying, "are your traditional chocolate chip, but I went with a particular brand of semi-sweet chocolate that I quite like, and the sea salt dusting—"

"YOU HAVE TO TRY THEM! THEY'RE SO GOOD!"

Maybe, I thought, it was like being at a rock concert. Maybe some temporary hearing damage would ensue. Maybe Fox and I didn't even need to worry about being quiet.

Once we were both inside the room, I drew on my gloves and shut the door. The study looked more or less the way it had when I'd been here the day before. There was no sign of fingerprint powder, no disarray that suggested a search. Maybe the sheriff or detective or whoever was in charge of this investigation had been careful to replace everything. Or maybe they hadn't gone through this room yet. Either way, it struck me as strange. Of course, they already thought they had the suspect in their sights (Hi! It's me!), so maybe they didn't feel the need for a comprehensive investigation.

We used the flashlights on our phones and navigated through the dark to Vivienne's desk, where the laptop, its screen dark, still sat. I gave Fox a questioning look. The giant, throne-like chair rolled easily as Fox adjusted it to sit, and they tapped a button on the laptop to power it up. As Fox set to work on the laptop, I knelt and began rifling the drawers.

I didn't know what we were looking for, not exactly. I knew that in any homicide investigation, the two principal elements to establish were motive and opportunity. Unlike a lot of mystery novels (and don't get me started on TV), actual investigations often took one as a jumping-off point for the other. Take my current predicament, for example. I was the prime suspect because I had opportunity—the secret passage into Vivienne's bedroom. For the moment, Sheriff Jakes couldn't explain my motive. I was fairly sure that was why I was listening to Indira and Millie become accessories (loudly)—

"I KNOW, RIGHT? IT'S CINNAMON!"

—instead of occupying a cell as the county jail's newest resident. And good police procedure (good investigative procedure in general, what Will Gower would have done) was to cast a wide net and then follow up on everything until you got somewhere. Knocking on doors, in urban police fiction. Or, in Golden Age mysteries, sifting cigar ash. That kind of thing.

As far as I knew, the only person (besides me) with the opportunity to kill Vivienne was her lawyer, Mr. Huggins. He'd been the last person to see her alive. And, if that slammed door was any indication, they hadn't parted on happy terms. But the problem with that was the problem of every locked-room mystery, and that's what this was: a real-life locked-room mystery. Vivienne had to be alive after Mr. Huggins left so that she could lock herself in her bedroom. Which meant, in theory, Mr. Huggins hadn't killed her. Of course, in locked-room mysteries, there was always a twist: the room wasn't actually locked, or not in the way you thought it was, or the person had died at a different time than you thought. In my case, the secret passage between our bedrooms seemed like the perfect solution to this particular locked-room mystery, but—since I was innocent—I needed to keep looking.

So, I was doing my best impersonation of Will Gower: I was going to try to gather all the information I could about Vivienne. And then I was going to follow the threads until I found something that helped me prove who had killed her.

Or until I was arrested. I squelched that thought.

The topmost drawers contained what you would expect: office supplies, stationery, a bonanza of stamps (if I ever needed to send snail mail, I knew where to go). For a moment, I wondered if this was a *Charade*-type situation, and maybe the stamps were priceless collectors' items. But a quick check of the USPS online store told me these were ordinary stamps.

The next drawer was one of the big ones, and it was locked. I frowned; bypassing locks of all kinds had been another dinnertime topic, but I wasn't sure I could get this open without leaving a mark. Then I remembered something. I reached past Fox to pull open the desk's center drawer. As soon as it slid out, the latch in the bottom drawer released, and it opened easily. Hanging folders held what appeared to be financial documents. I pulled out a few, tried to make sense of them, and immediately gave up. The numbers swam back and forth. I hadn't been lying when I'd told Vivienne my parents didn't have much business sense, and I was, after all, their child.

"Leave them," Fox whispered. "I'll take a look; I'm about to give up on this thing."

The lock screen on the laptop suggested Fox hadn't had any luck hacking Vivienne's account (and yes, I know I shouldn't have called it hacking—I'd once gotten a story shredded in a workshop for using the term too liberally, so now I use it out of general spite). I left the drawer with the financial papers open and moved to the drawers on the other side of the kneehole.

I found more hanging folders with what appeared to be correspondence— at least, the sheets of paper were folded like they'd once been in envelopes. I laid the first folder on the desk, with the thought of scanning the letters to see if anything suspicious jumped out at me, but I didn't get far. The first letter was a single sheet of loose-leaf, and someone had scrawled the words *I am going to get you* across the page. The writer had used a ballpoint pen with so much force that they'd torn the paper at the tail of the Y.

"Fox," I whispered.

Fox gave up on the laptop and turned their attention to the papers. Their eyes widened. After a moment, they slid the first letter off the stack and examined the next. It was similar, only the words said, *You will pay.* The one after that said, *You won't get away with this.* On and on like that. There had to be hundreds of them, all on loose-leaf, all done in blue ballpoint.

"My, my, my," Fox whispered. And then, eyebrows arched, "You didn't write these, did you?"

"What?" That was bordering on Millie-volume, so I lowered my voice. "Of course not."

Fox gave me a tiny grin.

Some of the tension in my body relaxed, and I managed to huff an amused breath. "That's not funny."

"This is good," they said. "As soon as the sheriff sees this, he's going to realize there's somebody else he should be looking at. This should get you off the hook."

I hadn't seen any envelopes to indicate who had sent these messages, and none of them was signed. I inched the folder closer to me and checked the organizer tab. I recognized the name written on it—I even recognized, to my surprise, Vivienne's elegant cursive. Matrika Nightingale, the tab said. My heart sank.

Anyone with even a passing interest in Vivienne Carver's work—or, for that matter, who had successfully lived through the Reagan era—would have recognized that name. Matrika Nightingale was a serial killer who had operated in Portland in the summer of 1987 and again in the summer of 1988. She'd killed four young women. And then she'd been caught by a young Vivienne Carver, whose first novel, *Death at Maplewood Manor*, had been published only the year before. The story of how Vivienne had met Nightingale had become a legend among mystery writers; it was the kind of thing that seemed like it had been lifted from the pages of one of Vivienne's own books. Vivienne had approached Nightingale for a research consultation. Vivienne was planning a new book, and she was considering a female ornithologist as the protagonist. But as Vivienne had met with Nightingale and gotten to know her, she had begun to suspect something was wrong. It was the first murder Vivienne ever solved, and it set her up for the rest of her career—not only as a writer (her second book, *The Riddle at Ravenhurst Hall*, was loosely based on the Nightingale Murders, and it broke bestseller records all over the world; and her nonfiction, true crime book *The Nightingale Murders* was nominated for a Pulitzer), but as a celebrity sleuth, traveling the world, solving crimes wherever she went.

So, if I'd had to pick a candidate for someone who would want to murder Vivienne, Matrika Nightingale would have been at the top of the list. Unfortunately, Nightingale was serving multiple life sentences at the Oregon

State Penitentiary, which meant she hadn't been in any position to kill Vivienne the night before. Hey, I thought, with a flicker of panicked hilarity, maybe Ms. Nightingale and I would be cellmates.

Fox must have understood too. When they saw the name on the folder, they grimaced. Then, without another word, they returned the folder to its place. They gave me a pat on the shoulder and rolled the chair over to inspect the financial documents.

I stared at the hanging folders with all those lovely, convenient death threats that were absolutely zero use to me. Then I shut the drawer. I opened the next one. More hanging folders. I flicked through them. No threats. No warning. No severed teddy bear heads or fingernail clippings or whatever obsessed fans sent their celebrity crush. Just more papers. Vivienne Carver had lived out her whole life on paper—in more ways than one.

It took me a few moments of rifling the papers (okay, of feeling sorry for myself) before I actually looked at the documents I was handling. They were a manuscript, I realized. A draft of a novel called *Café Capers*. The protagonist was a woman named Flossie Thorn who ran a cat café in a small ski town. She apparently had a lot of nice friends who did and said lots of nice things and everyone was nice and everything was nice. The first chapter consisted entirely of Flossie and her group of friends (called, I kid you not, the Golden Gang) complimenting each other for *gracefully embracing the beauty of their aging bodies.*

It wasn't like anything Vivienne had ever written, and apparently even she'd had her doubts—the original draft at the very back of the drawer was titled *Teahouse Tizzies,* and it seemed she'd considered a nom de plume, since the byline was different. The protagonist in that version wasn't called Flossie—she was called Dolly. And it wasn't a ski town, it was a spa town. But otherwise, the characters, the plot, even some of the dialogue—it was almost exactly the same. I couldn't keep myself from muttering, as I flipped through the manuscripts, "A penname was definitely the right choice."

Fox glanced over and frowned. "That's not a penname."

"Then who's Pippi Parker?"

"Pippi Parker? The author?"

"I have no idea who that is."

"She's a *New York Times*—" They stopped and waved at my phone. "Look her up."

It only took one search. Pippi Parker was, as Fox had said, a *New York Times*-bestselling author. In fact, almost all her books had made the list. She wrote cozies—cozy mysteries. And while I occasionally read cozies, and I enjoyed some of them, the genre wasn't one I'd been drawn to. My parents wrote much darker stories, and although I didn't tend to write anything quite as dark as theirs, I'd never found myself hooked by a cozy the way I'd been hooked by Lawrence Block or Adrian McKinty or, let's be real, Raymond Chandler.

The author photos of Pippi Parker showed a middle-aged white woman. She had platinum-colored hair in a volumized, layerized, electrified (that's probably not the right word) pixie cut, and it was immediately clear to me that this woman had never met an eye shadow she didn't like. She didn't look familiar to me, so I showed the photos to Fox.

"That's her."

"I don't get it," I said. "Were they friends or something?"

A laugh burst out of Fox before they could silence themselves. I would have been worried, but Millie's voice was still carrying clearly from the hall: "And that was the THIRD time I broke my arm! The FOURTH time—"

"They're definitely not friends," Fox whispered. "I don't know why she'd have this."

I glanced at *Teahouse Tizzies* again, and then I took a longer look at *Café Capers.* They were so similar. Too similar. And a part of me knew what that meant, but I was having a hard time wrapping my head around the fact that Vivienne Carver—the Vivienne Carver—would need to plagiarize anyone's story, much less Pippi Parker's. I mean, in one chapter, the characters spent ten pages giving each other back rubs.

"I need more time to look through this stuff," Fox said, waving at the financial documents. "But it looks like Vivienne spent a lot of money recently. Some kind of investment, I think, but as I said, I need some time to see what's really going on."

"Let's take pictures, and we'll leave the originals so the sheriff can look at them."

Fox raised one eyebrow; they were too polite to say *if the sheriff bothers to look at all.*

Between the two of us, it actually didn't take that long to photograph the financial paperwork. We returned everything to how we'd found it. As we crept back toward the door, Deputy Dairek said, "We'd better get back to work. The county doesn't pay me to stand around all night."

The female deputy murmured something that sounded like "It sure seems like it."

"One more for the road won't hurt," Deputy Dairek said.

"And you're eating it in the hall because I don't want to explain to the sheriff why there's pound cake in his crime scene."

"Leave the coffee too," Deputy Dairek said. "There's a good girl."

Indira didn't respond to that. I didn't know for a fact that Deputy Dairek was at a sudden risk of having Indira decapitate him with nothing but her bare hands, but to judge by the look on Fox's face, my guess probably wasn't far off.

As we reached the door, Millie said, "OH MY GOD, LOOK OVER THERE!"

Fox didn't hesitate. They pulled open the door and darted across the hall. I followed, easing the study door shut behind us. I had that panicked moment again, waiting for a board to creak, but we reached the bedroom without making a noise. There was something to be said, apparently, for being an insanely demanding robber-baron when it came to long-lasting home design.

In the darkness of the bedroom, Fox and I caught our breaths. Then we looped back around to the other side of the house and went down the servants' stairs. Indira and Millie were already in the kitchen: Indira washing up at one of the enormous sinks, and Millie sitting on the counter, swinging her legs.

"Well?" Millie asked. "Did we get anything?"

"I should call his mother," Indira said, waving a sudsy plate at us. "'There's a good girl.' He still lives with Gail, you know. She'd—she'd make him clean out the litter boxes."

Fox grinned at the confusion on my face and said, "Approximately a million cats."

"Oh my God," Millie said, "that was so scary. It was super scary. I was SO SCARED!"

It was hard to tell if she was serious since she had a mile-wide smile on her face.

"Well?" Indira said. "Tell me putting up with that buffoon was worth it."

"I think it was. Fox is going to work on some financial paperwork. Indira, maybe you could help."

"What about us?" Millie asked.

I wasn't sure about how quickly she'd made the jump to *us*, but honestly, I was so caught up in the night's discoveries that I said, "Tomorrow, I'm going to talk to Pippi Parker."

Chapter 7

At seven in the evening the next day, I parked the Jeep in the tiny lot of the Hastings Rock public library. Every spot was full, so I had to get creative, but I managed to make it work. Then I headed into the library.

It was a long, low building with hardboard siding and small windows, and it looked like it had been inspired by a shoebox. My guess was that it had been built (or at least commissioned) before Hastings Rock had established itself as a tourist destination, public funds being what they were. The evening was cool (of course), and although the day had been gray and drizzly, a rift had opened in the clouds, and sunset bathed the little town in gold. That sunny glow had tricked me again—my LEVEL UP T-shirt, shorts, and yes, the Mexico 66's weren't cutting it.

I assumed it was easier to enjoy the beauty of Hastings Rock when you weren't on the verge of hypothermia. The break in the weather had brought everyone out onto the streets again: a teenage boy lagging behind his family to take pictures of the ocean; a small crowd watching a busker do backflips; a kindly looking older woman comforting a crying little boy about a spilled ice cream cone. The woman was wearing a candy-striped apron, and it sounded like she was promising him a new one.

That made me smile; it had been a long day, with not much to smile about. Everything had started wonderfully with journalists thronging the gates to

Hemlock House—word of Vivienne's death had spread. And although they hadn't stopped me from coming and going, I was painfully aware of cameras flashing and reporters shouting questions, microphones pointed at the windows of the Jeep, as I eased through the crowd.

I'd tried to find Pippi earlier, and although it hadn't been hard to get her address (Hastings Rock wasn't that big, and between Millie and Fox, they knew pretty much everyone and everything), I hadn't had any luck when I'd visited her house. Then Sheriff Jakes had called and asked me to come into the station. He must have believed that a night spent tossing and turning and stewing in my own guilt would have softened me up for a confession, but the joke was on him. Instead of submitting myself to Sheriff Jakes's pleasant company yet again, I'd called a defense attorney in Portland and spent most of the day juggling phone calls from the attorney, the sheriff, and (of course) my parents—they'd been ghoulishly excited for me, in case you were wondering. Dad kept saying if there was a trial, they'd definitely fly out.

In between calls, I'd stalked Pippi as best I could. The internet didn't have much to say about her personal life except that she was "happily married to the best man in the world for the last twenty years (I love you, Stephen!)" and "keeps herself busy with three growing boys (Dylan, you're not my favorite—stop telling Christian you are)." It was interesting, though, to learn that she was, well, prolific. That seemed like the politest word for it. She churned out dozens of novels a year, writing across various series and pen names, none of which appeared to be a secret. The reviews were…ungenerous, let's put it. Especially of the more recent titles. And while she had slapped *New York Times Bestselling Author* on literally every available (digital) surface, it looked like that had been only one of her many series, and even that one had declined precipitously in sales.

But the most important thing I learned was that she was going to be doing a public reading from a new work tonight at the Hastings Rock public library. That's the beauty about authors—even though we'll all tell you we're introverts and we're shy and retiring and we don't like people, shine a spotlight, and we'll tear each other's wigs off to be the center of attention. The reading was announced on Pippi's author website, on her Facebook page, in her Facebook reader group, on Twitter, and—I now saw as I stepped into the library—on a flyer tacked to the library's bulletin board.

Inside, the library matched the exterior: economy carpeting, particleboard furniture, fluorescent lights. Even with lights, though, the space felt cramped and dim, mostly because of the tiny windows. It smelled like aging book glue and newspaper ink and the perpetual damp of a coastal town. And coffee. That perked me up a little, because if there was coffee, there might also be pastries, and I hadn't eaten since—God, I didn't know when I'd eaten today. I made my way past the circulation desk, past the children's section, following my nose toward a multipurpose room so crowded that any fire marshal worth his salt would have immediately shut the whole thing down. I found a spot along the back wall between a woman wearing enormous glasses (she had a Nordstrom bag between her feet, and it was full of Pippi Parker paperbacks) and, on my other side, a woman in a fedora and trench coat. She had an unfiltered (and, thank God) unlit cigarette hanging from the corner of her mouth. I found her, Sheriff Jakes, I wanted to say. I found the real killer.

I gave the room another glance—rows of chairs faced a temporary stage at the far end of the room, and every seat taken. On the stage, a rocking chair with a lace antimacassar and (no joke) another lace doily on the seat cushion sat next to a small end table. There was even an old-fashioned lamp. It felt like someone had picked the whole kit out of a grandmother's living room (a very frugal grandmother, mind you), and decided to use it as—what? A set?

Then I saw the coffee and, almost as importantly, the snacks. They were just the pre-wrapped kind, but my stomach still gave an enormous grumble. The woman with the glasses turned to look at me. The woman who was pretending to be Humphrey Bogart almost lost her cigarette. I squeezed out from between them, made my way to the coffee and snacks, helped myself to a

CHOCOLATE CAKE ROLL (compare to Hostess Ho Hos), and was in the middle of pouring myself some coffee when—

"Oh my God, DASH!"

And then a hug delivered at Mach 3.

And then coffee everywhere.

And then Dashiell Dawson Dane saying things that are not normally said in public, especially not in a library, especially not in front of a little white-haired lady in a sweater that said WORLD'S BEST GRANDMA.

"I'm sorry," I muttered as I sopped up coffee with a handkerchief.

"You need more variety," the grandma said. "You got stuck in a rut there in the middle."

"I'm sorry, I'm sorry, I'm sorry," Millie said as she tried to help. In the process, she managed to mash my chocolate cake roll (compare to Hostess Ho Hos), spill the rest of my coffee, and upend an open container of creamer in a truly miraculous way that spattered the left side of my jacket.

"It's okay," I said. "Millie, stop, it's fine." She didn't stop, in case you were wondering, but between the two of us, we managed to clean up most of the mess, and then we shuffled out of the way so a bug-eyed man could get some coffee. He gave us a particularly nasty look when he found the creamer container empty.

"This is so exciting," Millie stage-whispered. "I can't believe we're doing this!"

The *we* in that sentence was probably something I should have anticipated.

"Are we going to charge up there and demand that she answer some questions?" Millie asked. "Are we going to shout, STOP!"

Everyone stopped. A mom bouncing her baby on her knee stopped. A librarian in a chokingly tight cardigan stopped. Even the bug-eyed man stopped halfway back to his seat. The woman who had been playing Bogart actually put her hands in the air, and then she took two stumbling steps and broke into a run. Fortunately, aside from the Bogart lady, they all seemed to know Millie, and the hum of conversation and activity began again almost immediately. A few people, though, seemed to be giving me a second look, considering me as though trying to place me. One of them was a burly man, a lumberjack type, beard, flannel, muddy boots—the whole getup. Our eyes met, and I looked away first. When I risked another glance, he was still staring at me.

"No," I whispered, dragging Millie a little farther along the wall. I gave an apologetic half-wave to the rest of the room. "We're not going to do anything."

"We're just going to let her get away with it?" Millie asked. "That doesn't seem like a very good plan, especially since the sheriff thinks you did it."

"No, we—" I stopped. I drew in a deep breath. "How about this? How about we wait and see how things go?"

Millie frowned. Then she nodded. "Got it, boss."

"Oh God, I'm definitely not your boss—"

"Welcome, everyone, to our monthly Reading Room Reading." The librarian in the strait-jacket cardigan had made her way to the front of the room, and now she stood there, hands clasped as she waited for our silence. The room settled down quickly (these were, after all, people who chose to spend their free time in a library), and the librarian continued, "We're so happy to have you here. Tonight, we're excited to be hosting one of our own. Pippi Parker is a native of Hastings Rock, and until yesterday's tragedy, one of our two celebrity authors. Before we continue with tonight's event, I'd like to ask everyone to join me in a moment of silence for Vivienne Carver."

Maybe it was the mention of Vivienne's name, but during the moment of silence, several wandering eyes came my way again. Nobody seemed to be able to place me, not yet, but my face felt hot, and I knew it was only a matter of time.

After the moment of silence, the librarian continued with an introduction of Pippi. I listened carefully for anything I might have missed, but it was mostly broad statements with an abundance of goodwill behind them—how wonderful Pippi was, how talented, how insightful into the human condition. When the librarian had finished, everyone applauded as Pippi stood from the front row and made her way to the rocking chair. I fought a wave of the giggles as I realized that she was going to sit in the rocking chair as she did her reading. Story time for adults, I thought. And I realized maybe I needed something to eat, and maybe I needed more sleep, because I had a mental picture of all of us sitting on the story-time rug while Pippi read from her rocking chair, and I had to bite the inside of my cheek. Will Gower, I thought distantly, never had this problem. Will Gower was never hunkered in the sallow lighting of a gin joint, hand on his gat, fighting a fit of the tee-hees. Yet another way I was not Will Gower.

"I'm so grateful to be here tonight," Pippi said. She looked like the photos I'd seen online: the same pixie cut of platinum-colored hair, the same boxer's jaw, eye shadow the exact same color as a witch's poison. Her voice had a dollhouse affect, as though she'd spent most of her life working with small children. "Even though my heart is broken by the loss of my dear, dear friend Vivienne."

Millie gave an un-Millie like snort and whispered, "Real broken-up. I heard she spent all day getting splashed at a wine bar in Astoria. Like she was celebrating."

That was interesting, and I might have asked a follow-up except the bug-eyed man had turned in his seat to stare at us—it had been a Millie whisper, after all.

"But I know my beloved Vivienne would have wanted us to carry on. And so, tonight, I'd like to dedicate this reading to her memory." She turned her face up—either toward heaven or, just as likely, the water-stained acoustic tiles—and said, "We love you, Vivienne."

A murmur of gratification and approval rolled through the crowd. The bug-eyed man wiped his eyes. The woman with the Nordstrom bag burst into tears.

"Tonight, the work I've chosen to share with you is very special to me. This is a new story. Completely new, in fact. Nobody has seen it yet—not even my agent."

Another gratified murmur rippled through the audience.

"It's going to be the start of a new series, and let me tell you—" She leaned forward in the rocking chair, and her exaggerated whisper had the familiar hokeyness of old-school children's programming. "—it's going to be a knockout!"

Excitement. Thrills. A man in a wool tie pinched the woman next to him, which she didn't appear to appreciate.

"The working title is *Teahouse Tizzies*," Pippi said, "and I hope you enjoy it." She cleared her throat and began to read. "Dolly Ford was so very happy. It was the happiest time of her life. She looked around the room at her friends, who had gathered for their weekly session of tea and knitting. And she was so very happy. She had entered the fullness of the ripeness of her years with a deep, deep happiness—"

There was more, but I couldn't listen to it (take that however you will). My mind kept going back to three facts: first, Pippi was reading from *Teahouse Tizzies*; second, I'd found a manuscript of *Teahouse Tizzies* in Vivienne's desk; and third, most problematic, Pippi had told everyone that no one had seen this story before. And I knew that wasn't true—not only had Vivienne seen it, she'd stolen it.

But why lie about that? Why pretend no one had seen it if, at some point, she must have given Vivienne a copy? Was it simply to make the audience feel special? Pippi certainly seemed hopeful that this new series would buoy up her flagging career, but in that case, why not capitalize on the scandal of Vivienne's death? With Vivienne gone, Pippi could have told any story she wanted—that they were best friends, that they'd been collaborating, that her relationship with Vivienne had been the inspiration for Dolly's best friend—uh, I wanted to say her name was Ruth. Maybe that would have seemed a little shameless, but what was I supposed to expect from a woman who brought her own lamp to an author reading?

I was so caught up in my thoughts that I didn't realize the reading had ended until applause broke out. The librarian in the disturbingly form-fitting cardigan stood near Pippi's rocking chair and said, "We'll now open the floor to questions."

Hands shot into the air.

Millie's hand shot into the air.

I had a single instant to think: *Millie, no.*

I tried to grab her wrist and pull her hand back down, but it was like a nightmare, and I was so slow.

"Let's see—" the librarian tried.

"Did you kill Vivienne?" Millie asked.

The question sucked all the air out of the room. Nobody moved. I was intensely aware of Pippi in that moment. That was a trauma response, part of my brain informed me. Hyperprocessing sensory input. Everything clear and frozen like a photograph. Pippi's lips parted. That boxer's jaw sagged. Her cheeks slackened, and then a hint of color rose in them.

She burst out laughing.

The sound seemed to release everyone else. Murmurs ran through the crowd. A baby began to cry. The bug-eyed man turned in his seat to glare at Millie and mouth, *How dare you?*

But Pippi kept laughing. She rocked once in her chair, like this was so much fun, and then, through her laughter, said, "Oh my goodness, no."

Her voice still held that dollhouse quality, that porcelain preschool affect. But her eyes had hardened, and the red in her cheeks was more pronounced. She stood, and the rocking chair rocked behind her. She scanned the crowd, clearly seeking out the source of the question. When she saw us, she put her hands on her hips. "Honestly, Millie, I'm hurt that—ah ha!"

If you've never heard someone say, *Ah ha!* in real life before, you're missing out. It's simultaneously unbelievable and amazing. It was slightly less amazing when Pippi's arm shot out, and she pointed straight at me. "I see what's going on here. Ladies and gentlemen, we have someone special with us here tonight. Allow me to present Dashiell Dane, the man who murdered Vivienne Carver."

Gasps. Shock. A little old lady shook her fist at me. The lumberjack on the far side of the room shifted his weight and started breathing loudly. The word that came to mind was stentorian.

"I didn't—" I tried.

"He didn't kill her," Millie said, and this time, her standard Millie volume was an asset because her voice carried clearly over the crowd. "We're trying to figure out who did, and we think maybe you did because—" Millie stopped. And then, without any apparent hesitation at the treachery, she said, "Tell them, Dash," and pushed me forward.

It was only one staggering step, but it carried me into a clearing in the aisle, and I felt every eye in the library on me. (Two particularly buggy eyes, for the record, were looking particularly hateful.) "You know what?" I said. "There's been a misunderstanding—"

"The misunderstanding," Pippi said over me, "is why the sheriff hasn't arrested you yet. Did you know Vivienne offered this man a job? She took him into her house, gave him shelter under her roof, and to pay back that kindness, he pushed her out her window."

"Technically, I think it was the balcony," I said, which I realized, in hindsight, wasn't as helpful as it had sounded in my head.

"Someone grab him!" a frightened voice called from the audience.

A man shouted, "Call the sheriff!"

Pippi had a strange expression on her face, and it took me a moment to recognize it: she was trying not to smile. "He hated Vivienne, you understand," she said, and there was something so stagey about her voice, so artificial, so purposefully projected, that I looked around—and that's when I saw the man in the front row who was recording her on his phone. It was a show, I realized. The whole thing was a show. "He hated her because she was talented and successful and a brilliant writer. And he hated her because he can't write anything himself."

For a moment, the only thing I could think was: how? How had she learned that? How did she even know who I was? I'd barely been in Hastings Rock a couple of days, and I hadn't even known Pippi's name until the night before. How could she know anything about me, much less something about my writing?

But that confusion only lasted a moment before anger surged up, and I said, "I barely knew Vivienne. I certainly didn't hate her, and I did not murder her." Rage swept away my hesitating and procrastinating and indecision. The words came to me the way they did when I was doing my best writing, when everything seemed to flow. It was like I could hear Will Gower saying them: in a high-rise apartment, the windows lashed by rain, a crowd of suspects gathered for the dramatic reveal. "When did you learn Vivienne had stolen your story?"

Shock cracked Pippi's mask. She gathered herself, but her words were stumbling when she said, "I don't know what you're talking about."

"Of course you do. There are dozens of drafts of *Café Capers* in Vivienne's desk. A forensic analysis will show that she lifted the plot and characters from *Teahouse Tizzies*. Your new book wasn't a secret project that nobody else saw. Vivienne saw a copy, and I think I know why. You took it to Vivienne because you needed help. Because your books weren't selling. And Vivienne turned around and stole it. You and Vivienne weren't friends. In fact, you didn't like each other, and I imagine lots of people can testify to the fact you and your beloved Vivienne were always at each other's throats. Two authors living in the same small town. Two authors with big egos. Two authors who write such different kinds of stories. Only you never had Vivienne's success. You never had the TV show, the celebrity status." I spared her a slice of a grin. "You never solved a real murder. So, I'm curious: when did you learn she was plagiarizing your work? Did you blackmail her? Did you threaten her? Did she refuse to pay, and things got out of hand?"

Terror tightened Pippi's face, compressing her features until she looked older than her years. Her voice cracked as she shouted, "I have an announcement!"

Again, it's a treat if you've never experienced it in person.

"I have an announcement," she said again. "I didn't want to share this until I'd spoken to Vivienne's family, but I'm going to tell you now because—because this horrible man is desecrating her memory. Yes, Vivienne and I had our differences. But we respected each other. We shared a love of the craft. And, by the end, we loved each other like sisters. I'm proud to announce that *Teahouse Tizzies* and *Café Capers* are sister novels, and they are a co-written project by Vivienne Carver and Pippi Parker. Vivienne's last work. And also her greatest. It was an honor to work with a talent of such literary genius, and I'm excited for everyone to see what two great writers working together can accomplish. Vivienne, this book is for you."

"Good Lord," Millie said under her breath.

Excited conversation broke out among the crowd. One man was clutching a Pippi Parker paperback to his chest like he was about to swoon. The white-haired lady who had commented on my swearing was trying to take a picture of me with her iPad. The lumberjack, still staring at me, was breathing harder.

"And to honor my friend and creative partner," Pippi said, "I will assume the mantle of Matron of Murder. Vivienne's life work was the pursuit of justice, in her stories and in the world. There can be no greater tribute than for me to take up her torch and continue that work. And to begin, I vow to you, Vivienne—" This was directed to the water stain again. "—that I will not rest until I have helped the sheriff convict this man of your murder."

"You have got to be kidding me," I said.

"And I will be offering an exclusive patrons-only podcast about my investigation into my best friend's murder and my work as the new Matron of

Murder to patrons at the Pippi's Pep Rally tier and above. Please consider signing up for the full year to provide me with the financial support I need to pursue my creative dream. Er, justice for Vivienne."

"Do you have a QR code?" a man asked, waving his hand frantically from the audience.

Millie was agape. When she looked at me, she said, "That woman does not miss a trick."

Somehow, I managed to say, "Let's get out of here. This is insane."

But as I took a step toward the door, Pippi called out "Not so fast! For my first dramatic revelation, ladies and gentlemen, I will reveal Dashiell Dane's motive for murdering Vivienne."

"You already revealed my motive," I said as I ushered Millie toward the exit. "You told everyone I hated her because I'm a failure at writing."

"But killing Vivienne wasn't enough for you, was it? You had to have more. You had to have everything. And, in order to have it, you had to get rid of Vivienne."

"I didn't—"

"Ladies and gentlemen, I discovered today—to my horror and chagrin and ultimate outrage—that Dashiell Dane is Vivienne's sole heir."

It was like something vast came down and crushed every sound in an instant. There was a slight, thunderous echo that might have been only in my head. I couldn't seem to keep moving; even Millie looked rooted to the floor.

"No," I said. "That's not—"

"It's true," Pippi said over me. "My source at the county recorder's office confirmed that Mr. Dane is the new owner of Hemlock House. I'm sure the sheriff will be both interested and grateful when I share this information with him."

Grateful wasn't the word I would have chosen, I thought dully. Gleeful, maybe. Because even though I had no idea how what Pippi was saying could be true, if it was true, it could only mean one thing: I had a rock-solid motive for murdering Vivienne Carver. And until now, a lack of motive was the only thing that had kept the sheriff from arresting me.

CHAPTER 8

Somehow, we made it out of the library. I'd expected outrage, clutching hands, cries of "Murderer!" But aside from a few dirty looks, most people had seemed more interested in Pippi's new podcast and patronage platform. When Millie and I emerged into the night, the crowds of tourists had already dried up, and the shops were shuttered, and the town was cold and dark. A few stars showed out to the west. Fog was moving in, and the air was wet against my face.

"It's a misunderstanding," Millie said. "She got it wrong somehow."

I nodded.

"Fox and Indira will know what to do. You'll see."

"Right," I said.

"Dash, are you okay?"

No, I wanted to say. I'm about to be arrested, and I've got a lunatic master of self-promotion who's going to make sure I go to prison for a murder she very well could have committed.

But Will Gower wouldn't have said that; he would have said something dry, something wry, something that would have made Millie roll her eyes but, at the same time, reassured her that he had everything in hand. I wasn't Will Gower, as tonight's disastrous confrontation had proven, but in this moment Dashiell Dane and Will Gower weren't that far apart. Because Dashiell Dane wouldn't say something like that either. Dashiell Dawson Dane was much more likely to say exactly what I said next: "Oh sure. Fine."

Millie frowned and gave me a considering look.

"Really," I said and managed a smile. "Thank you for—" Uh, accusing someone of murder in public and escalating a terrifying confrontation didn't really sound right, so I settled for "—the help tonight."

"You don't look like you're fine. You look like when my mom and I are talking and then my mom gets a headache and then my mom says she needs to lie down for a while."

There was a lot to unpack in that sentence; weirdly, it made it easier to let out a little laugh. "No, really. I think I'm just a little shaken up from—I mean, I don't understand." I wrestled down a secondary wave of panic and managed to say, "You're right. It's got to be some sort of mistake."

"We'll figure it out."

That made my eyes mist. I nodded. "I think I'd better call it. I've done enough damage for one night."

It looked like Millie might ask another question, but instead, with a flash of a smile, she hugged me. "See you tomorrow, Dash," she said and darted off toward her car.

When I got to the Jeep, there was a familiar envelope under windshield wipers. I didn't even bother opening it; now that I wasn't in such a rush, I spotted the fire hydrant. And the red curb. And the sign that said NO PARKING.

At least they hadn't towed the Jeep, I thought as I got in and started the engine. That was a win, right?

I started back toward Hemlock House, but my mind wasn't really on the route. I kept thinking back to Pippi's performance. How flashy it had been. How quickly she'd adapted. She hadn't liked it that I'd known Vivienne had plagiarized *Café Capers*. But was it a secret worth killing over? After that performance, I certainly didn't trust Pippi, but she seemed more focused on self-aggrandizement and profiting off a tragedy than, well, murderous.

And how in the world could I be Vivienne's sole heir? What did that even mean? I had an idea of what the estate must be worth—the intellectual property alone would be worth millions, not to mention whatever other assets Vivienne had. And owner of Hemlock House? That didn't make any sense. How could the county recorder of records have me listed as the new owner when Vivienne had only died two days ago? Didn't everything have to go through probate?

It didn't matter; that was the stopping point in my brain. None of it really mattered because I was never going to inherit anything. The slayer rule, it was called. You can't inherit from a person you killed. That's the kind of thing you knew if you were a mystery writer. Which raised a tickle at the back of my brain—why would I kill Vivienne if I knew about the slayer rule? I suppose law enforcement would assume I had believed I would never be caught, but still, it seemed like—well, my writer brain said it seemed like a plot hole.

And then it hit me: someone was framing me. I hadn't put it to myself in those words yet. Hadn't thought it out all the way. But as soon as it came to me, I understood: I was being framed. Vivienne's death the night I arrived, that wasn't a coincidence or bad luck. The sheriff finding that secret passage—that wasn't his savvy detecting skills. And now this, the fact that I was somehow Vivienne's heir and the owner of Hemlock House. Someone was making sure I took the fall for Vivienne's murder.

The crunch of gravel jerked me out of my thoughts, and I came back to myself as the Jeep veered off the road. Fortunately, the streets were empty. I yanked the wheel and straightened out my course, but I was shaking so badly that the Jeep swerved back and forth. Somehow, I managed to come to a stop on the shoulder. I killed the engine. And then I pressed my hands against my thighs, sucking in deep breaths, as panic burned a bright wick up to the center of my brain.

After a while, I got control of myself again. I thought about how this would sound when I told people about it, about how tonight would be something to laugh about—Pippi's staginess, her barefaced avarice, God, the podcast. But tonight, turning into a story didn't help all that much. I thought about Will Gower and what he'd do. For most of my life, I'd lived and breathed and dreamed with Will Gower. Will Gower's world-weary eye, taking in the foibles of the people he met. Will Gower's unflinching compassion, in spite of the world's darkness. Will Gower, who was never afraid. Never afraid to fail. Never afraid to let himself get hurt.

And I was not Will Gower.

Before I knew what I was doing, I reached for my phone and called Hugo. It only rang once before my brain caught up with my body. Then I punched the screen to end the call.

I had just wanted to hear a familiar voice, I told myself.

The phone vibrated in my hand, and Hugo's name appeared on the screen. I dismissed the call. The phone vibrated again a moment later with a voicemail. I didn't want to listen to it. He'd be kind. He'd understand. He'd listen. He'd be Hugo. And, because he was Hugo, he'd call again if he didn't hear back from me. So, I texted him: *Sorry about that.* And then, to prevent any further idiocy, I pocketed the phone.

The worst of the shaking had stopped, although I could feel my own unsteadiness. Something I could use in my writing, I thought. Something I could use to make Will Gower's descriptions more vivid. Every muscle weak. A bone-deep exhaustion. And an awareness that I was holding myself together with spit and twine. I stared out the windshield. I thought about the long drive through the dark tunnel of the spruce forest. I thought about the winding fog belt. I thought about the dark house on the sea cliffs, and the dark halls, and the dark room, and I thought about all the shadows moving inside Hemlock House.

My eyes refocused on the building ahead of me. Until now, I'd been focused on stopping the Jeep—and not freaking out—and so I hadn't registered what was right in front of me. The neon signage read THE OTTER SLIDE, and a pride flag drooped in the wet air. A bar, my brain said. Perfect.

Before I could consider if this was a good idea, I yanked the key from the ignition and got out of the Jeep. The bar itself was a single-story building with a built-up roof and shiplap siding. The large front windows had been blacked out at some point, which I took to be either a really good sign or a really bad one, depending on where the night was headed. Bud Light banners hung on the walls, in case you hadn't figured out what kind of place it was—and admittedly, a name like the Otter Slide conjured up all sorts of possibilities. In other places, the walls were papered with sun-faded ads for Miller, Corona, and, one I hadn't heard of before, Rock Top Brewing.

When I stepped inside, it looked…normal. A long bar took up one side of the room, with stools and taps and shelves lined with bottles. Track lighting lit the bar itself, but the rest of the space was pleasantly murky under pendant lights with gold and green glass. A handful of white guys were playing pool. An older woman who looked Native American was reading a book in a booth. Two kids—I mean, honestly, they must have barely turned twenty-one—were playing a pinball machine that looked like you were trying to shoot the balls up Darth Vader's nose. Of his mask, I mean. The smell of fried onions and malt hung in the air, and the music sounded like classic rock, although not too loud. I don't know why that surprised me, and then I did—a part of me had been expecting sea shanties. But the thing I couldn't help focusing on was that everywhere—everywhere—were stuffed animals. Little ones. Beanie Babies, and Beanie Baby knockoffs, and ones that were clearly from Japan. A little gay bear was nestled into a bowl that had clearly been designed for bar mix. A unicorn straddled one of the pendant lights. And an otter, of course, sat with legs splayed next to the top-shelf hooch.

I made my way over to the bar and took a stool, and a few seconds later, a woman drifted over to me. She looked like she was the only one working the bar tonight, and she had one of those energetic faces, tan from being outdoors and starting to collect a few lines, that was attractive without being beautiful. "Welcome to the Otter Slide," she said. "What can I get you?"

"A gimlet," I said.

"You don't hear that one too often. Coming right up."

She drifted back down the bar, mixed the drink, and brought it back. "Long day?"

I shook my head.

Like good bartenders everywhere, she knew when to leave someone with their drink. "Anything else I can get you?"

I needed food, but that took too much brain power, so I shook my head.

"Call me if you need anything," she said. "Name's Seely."

I nodded, and Seely left me to my drink. I'm not sure I like gimlets, for the record. I mean, I like them well enough to drink them. But what I really like is the…resonance, I guess. The echo. Philip Marlowe drinks gimlets. There's a whole scene of him drinking gimlets, and the first time I read it, I had no idea what it meant. But the sound of it, the way the phrase *gimlet eyes* had hung around the back of my head, the feeling of rightness—that this was a drink for cynical men in a cynical world—had stuck with me. Sometimes the lime made my teeth ache, though, in case anyone's wondering.

I had one gimlet. I had another. I ordered a third. My face felt flushed and my body loose, and I kept taking off my glasses and blinking to clear my eyes, even though a distant part of me was fairly certain my eyes weren't the problem. I knew I should definitely eat something, but the thought of making a decision—any decision—at this point seemed impossible. I thought about Vivienne, and Pippi, and the thrill in my mother's voice when she asked, *They arrested you?* I thought about Will Gower and the dark streets he walked alone. I thought about the impossible fact that I owned Hemlock House, and that I was Vivienne's heir. It had to be a mistake. In fact, I was going to tell the sheriff it was a mistake. I was going to tell him right now.

After dropping some cash on the bar, I stood. Or tried to. The bar slipped away. And the floor slipped away. I grabbed the stool, but the stool slipped too, and I would have taken it with me as I fell except a pair of strong hands caught me. They steadied me. The eyes that met mine were a rich, earthy bronze I'd only seen once before.

"Whoa," Deputy Bobby said. "You okay?"

"Whoa," I said, fighting a giggle. "Like a horse."

"Uh huh." He considered me for another moment. "Did you have something to drink, Mr. Dane?"

"My name is Dash. I told you to call me Dash." I wrested myself free of his grip—well, I tried to. It felt more like him politely releasing me, with one hand still hovering close in case I started to go over again. I straightened as best I could. I had a few inches on him, which was good. "I own Hemlock House. Did you know that?"

Something I couldn't read crossed his face. He said, "Why don't we sit down?"

"And everyone thinks I killed Vivienne. Everyone. Even you."

"I—"

"And you gave me—" I fumbled in my pocket because I was sure I had one on me somewhere. "—parking tickets!"

"Mr. Dane—"

"Lots of parking tickets! And that's rude!"

"Why don't we—"

"And I didn't kill anyone!"

Even through the gimlet haze, I was aware of my volume, my words carrying over the sound of "Another Brick in the Wall." People turned to look. Conversations faltered. Seely stood at the bar, watching us.

Deputy Bobby waved at her. Then he wrapped one of those strong hands around my arm and said, "I don't think you want to be yelling about something like that in public."

"Maybe I do. Maybe I want to tell everyone."

"Do you?"

The beat of the song pounded in time with the ache in my head. I dropped my gaze and mumbled, "No."

"We're going to sit down," Deputy Bobby said. "And you're going to drink some water and have something to eat."

It didn't seem like a question, so I let Deputy Bobby lead me over to an empty booth. He told me not to go anywhere, which was funny since the floor was definitely too slippery for me to get out of here on my own. I wasn't sure how long he was gone, but I heard him before I saw him.

"He's not my responsibility," Deputy Bobby was saying in the low voice of someone trying not to be overheard—and trying not to argue. "I'm just going to make sure he gets home safely."

The only answer was a sigh.

"I'm sorry," Deputy Bobby said.

The voice that answered was male, and something about the pitch sounded gay. "I know. You're always sorry."

Deputy Bobby didn't say anything to that, but his silence was impressively loud. He slid into the booth a moment later and set a glass of water and a basket of fries in front of me. Then another man slid in next to him. He was gorgeous; that was the only word for him. Pink-cheeked and pouty lipped, with flaxen hair in a disheveled side part and eyes the color of morning. He was also dressed for a night out: a cropped graphic tee that showed a sexy devil in a reclining pose; an expensive-looking bracelet, with an even more expensive-looking necklace; and I was fairly sure I'd glimpsed leather pants that I never in my life could have pulled off. I took another look at Deputy Bobby and realized he wasn't in his khaki uniform—he was wearing a colorful print button-up with the sleeves cuffed at the elbow. He had nice arms, I realized. A moment later, I realized I was staring, and they were staring at me staring, and I wondered how many more gimlets it would take to kill me.

"Hi," the newcomer said. "I'm West."

"I'm Dash," I said. "Sorry."

"Eat some fries," Deputy Bobby said.

"I'm going to tell everyone I met you," West said.

Deputy Bobby made a quick, pained face that vanished almost immediately.

"The girls are going to be so jealous."

"Um," I said, "yay?"

That seemed like my cue that talking was not, at present, my strong suit, so I jammed some fries in my mouth. They were hot, but not too hot. Salty, but not too salty. Crispy until all of a sudden you got to the delicious fluffiness of the potato inside. I moaned.

West burst out laughing.

"The fries are very good here," Deputy Bobby said with a grin.

"They're not that good," West said through his laughter. "If they tasted like that, I wouldn't need a boyfriend."

I took a drink of water and said, "This is a gay bar."

"It's gay-friendly," Deputy Bobby said. "Hastings Rock is too small for a proper gay bar."

West rolled his eyes. "It's a gay bar in everything but name. They even have a drag brunch once a month."

"Lots of locals drink here," Deputy Bobby said. "The drinks are reasonably priced, there aren't too many tourists, and the vibe is chill."

The words popped out of my mouth before I could stop them: "Did Deputy Bobby say the vibe is chill?"

West laughed again. "Deputy Bobby. Oh my God, like a cartoon or something."

And then, because the gimlets had only worsened my natural tendency to stick my foot in my mouth, I said, "Why are you in a gay bar?"

West started laughing so hard that Deputy Bobby actually gave him a look. But it didn't slow West down at all, and finally Deputy Bobby turned back to me and said, "Well, I'm gay. West is my boyfriend."

"Why are you in a gay bar?" West asked through tears of laughter.

"All right," Deputy Bobby said.

The heat in my face had nothing to do with the gimlets now, but weirdly, I actually felt better about the gaffe because…well, because I thought I'd felt something. Just a little. And it was nice to know I hadn't been wrong. And I liked it, too, when West kept laughing and Deputy Bobby gave me a crooked smile. Like we were both in on it together, whatever it was. Dealing with West maybe. Like we were on the same side.

"Oh my God, there's Jeremy," West said. "I'm gonna go dance. Nice to meet you, Dash."

He was gone in a heartbeat. And I'd been right about the leather pants.

The music had changed. I thought maybe this song was by The Doors, but I couldn't name it. Deputy Bobby sat there, watching me. And I sat there, uncomfortably aware of being watched. The silence between us stretched out. The shirt fit him perfectly across the shoulders. Broad shoulders. It was tight enough to hint at the definition of his chest.

"Eat," Deputy Bobby said. "You need something in your stomach besides—what were you drinking?"

"Gimlets."

He made a face and nudged the fries toward me.

So, I ate. And I drank water. And Seely brought me a hamburger, which was, honest to God, the best thing I've ever eaten in my whole life. I started to feel more like myself, which meant both tremendously embarrassed and extremely headachey.

I was about two bites away from finishing the hamburger when I said, "Thank you."

Deputy Bobby smiled. "You're welcome."

"Did I really look that bad?"

His laugh was low and easy, and he shook his head. "I was going to leave you alone. It looked like you wanted your privacy." That wry grin surfaced again. "And parking tickets tend to make things awkward."

I groaned.

"There was a fire hydrant."

"I know, I know."

"But I was going to get us more drinks when you got a little unsteady—"

"You mean when I fell. Drunkenly. Into your arms."

Now that last part—that wasn't supposed to be there. But Deputy Bobby only laughed again.

"I promise I'm alright," I said. "You don't have to play babysitter." I tried to stop there, but I couldn't help myself. "You're ruining your date with West. I guess technically I'm ruining it."

"It's not a date when you live together; he wanted to go out, so we went out. And West understands."

But I wasn't sure about that. I'd heard West's sigh. I'd heard the defensiveness in Deputy Bobby's voice when he hadn't known I was listening.

I wasn't prepared for the directness of the question, for the honesty behind it, the sincerity. "Are you all right?"

My eyes stung. I tried to nod, but somehow I ended up shaking my head instead. "Yes," I said. "No. I don't know."

He waited. Then he said, "That mostly covers it. Want to talk about it?"

"No. God, no." I tore the edge off the remaining piece of lettuce on my burger, and the words burst out of me. "If I were halfway decent as a mystery writer, I'd be able to figure this out, you know."

Deputy Bobby started to smile. He must have realized I wasn't joking, though, because the expression faded. "There's a difference between telling a story about a homicide and actually investigating one. That might not be a popular opinion around here, but it's true."

"Vivienne did it. Pippi's going to do it—well, I mean, it'll be a travesty and a miscarriage of justice, but she'll still make a ton of money off of it and become an overnight celebrity. My parents could do it. And I can't even decide if Will Gower is going to have a campy, flirtatious secretary with an on-again-off-again romance or if he's going to be a brooding lone wolf whose only emotional connection is the kid he plays chess with."

He frowned. "Is that a friend of yours?"

"And do you know what the worst part is? If my parents were here, they'd already have figured the whole thing out."

"Are your parents police officers?"

"What? No, they're writers. But they would have. They're both unbelievably smart. They'd love this. The whole thing would be a romp for them. They'd get into all sorts of shenanigans and figure it all out in a few hours and have a great time. Me, on the other hand? I chased down one lead—one!— and somehow it made me look even guiltier!" I had to blink to clear my eyes, and I took a drink to try to loosen the strain in my voice. "It would be nice, just once, if I weren't such a disappointment. Not that they can be bothered to be disappointed. They'd have to take an interest to be disappointed. Hey, maybe that'll be a bright spot about prison. Mom and Dad will love visiting because they'll have so many questions about shanks and shivs and toilet wine."

In the wake of the words, I felt hollow. My joints ached. My head was throbbing. The food, which had tasted so good going down, now sat in a greasy lump in my stomach. Deputy Bobby was staring at me with a look I'd once seen on a tourist when a seagull had screamed right in his face.

"I'm sorry," I said. "That was a lot, and I shouldn't have—I'm really sorry."

I slid out of the booth, managed to find some more cash to throw on the table for the fries and burger, and fled.

The wet air had finally thickened into a drizzle, and my glasses were immediately useless. I started off for the Jeep. I was still a little unsteady from the gimlets, and the gravel sloshed underfoot, making every step a balancing act.

I shouldn't have run out of the bar. I shouldn't have left at all. I should have stayed, laughed off my own words, robbed the moment of that vital charge of emotion that had left me exposed and vulnerable. I should have found a way to turn it all into a story. To turn it into a joke.

Gravel crunched again behind me, and I glanced back. A dark shape approached through the drizzle, and with my glasses wet, I couldn't make out anything but a shape.

"You aren't driving yourself home," Deputy Bobby said. He came closer, and I could make out the shape of his face. "Not unless you want to add a DUI on top of all those parking tickets."

"I wasn't—" But, of course, I was. And then I tried "I'm not—"

"Keys."

"But West—"

He held out his hand.

I wiped my glasses and got a blurry look at his face. I was starting to suspect Deputy Bobby didn't get mad or excited or out of sorts. I was starting to think Deputy Bobby operated at a baseline of unflappable, earnest seriousness, and for some reason, it made me think of Hugo, charming, beautiful Hugo, who was always exactly whoever you wanted him to be. I fished out my keys.

Deputy Bobby walked me to the passenger side, ignoring me when I insisted I was fine, and he helped me up into the Jeep. He went around and got behind the wheel. The Jeep started up, and he took a moment to check the wipers and the lights, and then the tires bit into the gravel, and we merged onto the road.

I leaned my cheek against the glass. My breath fogged it, and on the other side, rainwater beaded like jewels. Not long, and the forest closed around us. I couldn't smell the trees, though. I smelled my wet clothes, my wet hair. And something else. A hint of something that curled up in my belly and smoldered.

"I'm sorry," I said again. "I didn't mean to unload on you like that."

"If you want to talk about it, we can talk about it," Deputy Bobby said. "If you don't, we won't."

"That is way too simple," I said.

He laughed.

"I don't want to talk about it."

"Okay."

"I changed my mind."

His grin was a white slice in the night.

Maybe it was the gimlets. Maybe it was the burger and fries. Maybe it was simply that I was lonely, and for the second time, Deputy Bobby was giving me a ride home. I smiled back, and the smile surprised me. He was a stranger. And the rational part of my brain knew that he worked for the sheriff, that his current professional focus was proving that I killed Vivienne and making sure I went to prison for a long time. But it didn't feel like that.

I was, however, a notoriously bad judge of—I almost said men, but that made it sound like this, whatever it was, was something different. Bad at relationships, maybe. Although that didn't sound much better. Bad at peopling? That came close. I forced myself to sit up, to shake off whatever it was I was feeling, and to remember who he was and who I was and what exactly was going on (even though I wasn't entirely clear on that last part myself).

"How are you going to get home?"

"West will pick me up."

I remembered, again, the sound of West's sigh, the tone of Deputy Bobby's voice. "I'm sorry if, uh, I caused a problem."

"You didn't cause a problem." The Jeep wasn't exactly a quiet vehicle, and for a while, driving through the dark, the sound of the engine and the wind and the tires swallowed everything up. And then, with a hint of that tone I remembered, he added, "Honestly, he's probably having a better time without me."

"I'm sorry," I said again.

"Don't be."

The headlights splashed over ferns and moss and stone that was dark with water. The rain was still hovering at a drizzle, and the windshield wipers scraped back and forth. I hadn't realized how cold I'd been, but now the heat was loosening up my body. Everything was starting to feel far off. That spectacularly awful scene at the library, which actually had only been an hour or so ago, seemed like a dream. Well, a nightmare.

"I didn't kill her and steal her house," I said.

"You told me."

"I'm adding the part about the house. And about being her sole heir."

He made a noise that could have meant anything.

"Did you already know that part," I asked, "or am I giving you even more reasons to build a case against me?"

"Are you asking me to comment on an ongoing investigation?"

"Yes. I want you to tell me everything and then help me destroy the evidence."

Another of those grins. They were surprisingly goofy on someone who looked so serious most of the time.

"Is that a no?" I asked.

"Not tonight."

"No, that's more second date material." The words were out of my mouth (in true Dashiell fashion) before I could stop them, and then I let out a horrified, "I didn't mean that!"

Deputy Bobby burst out laughing.

"Oh my God," I said.

"It's fine. I knew what you meant."

That was good, because I didn't. But all I could come up with was "You need to arrest me now. You need to arrest me and throw me in jail and not let me talk to real people ever again because I'm clearly a menace to society."

He made that noise again, the one with a million possible meanings.

"This is entrapment," I told him. "That's what this is. I should call my lawyer."

"You should have a lawyer," he said, the playfulness dropping away. "That was smart; that was the right thing to do."

I opened my mouth to—what? Thank him for being supportive of me fighting a murder charge? But then a connection flashed in my brain, and I said, "The lawyer. I should call that lawyer!"

"What—"

"Higgins or Hitchens or Huggins—Huggins!" I took out my phone with the vague idea of doing a search for his information. "I have to talk to him. He'll know—I mean, he's Vivienne's lawyer, right? He'll know about the will and about the deed to Hemlock House. He'll be able to explain that it's a big misunderstanding. There was a mistake somehow. Something went wrong."

Deputy Bobby gave me a look, and now his mouth was a firm line, his expression closed off.

"What?" I said. "You don't think I should?"

He was quiet for what felt like a long time. The roar of the Jeep filled my head until I couldn't hear anything else. Then he said, "I think you're within your rights to talk to Mr. Huggins. In fact, I'm surprised he hasn't contacted you yet; as the executor of Vivienne's trust, he'll be in regular contact with you for a while, actually, since he'll be helping you with the transfer of assets."

"Then what's with the look?"

Another of those stretched-out silences came. Then, adjusting his hands on the steering wheel, he said, "It's a little late to call him tonight, don't you think?"

It was after nine, which yes, was probably late enough that Mr. Huggins wouldn't appreciate a phone call. But that hadn't been what Deputy Bobby had been about to say.

"If he knows how this happened—this mix-up, I mean—then maybe he can help us figure out who killed Vivienne." I wasn't sure how that *us* had slipped into my sentence, but there it was. "I'm going to call him first thing in the morning."

We turned in at the massive gates to Hemlock House. Above us, the manor was a dark bulk against the sky, and I thought again about the dark halls and dark rooms and dark secrets of that big, brooding house. As Deputy Bobby started up the hill, his attention appeared to be fixed on the drive, but his voice was tight when he said, "Mr. Dane, I'm going to say this as politely as I know how."

"That's never a good start."

"It would be best for you—and I truly mean that—to let the sheriff's office handle this investigation. Asking questions, stirring people up, that's not going to help you. In fact, it's making you look like you have something to hide."

"Trying to prove I'm innocent means I look guilty? Is that what you're telling me?"

Tension stiffened his jaw.

"Because everyone is entitled to a defense. And frankly, I don't care how it makes me look."

"Did you consider—"

"Yes, I did consider the possibility that you and the rest of the sheriff's office might be good at your jobs. I think you probably are. But it's my life. I'm the one on the hook for this murder, and as far as I can tell, the sheriff doesn't seem interested in looking at anyone else. You'll have to excuse me if I try to save my own neck; I'm sorry if that doesn't look good to the rest of Hastings Rock."

"I was going to say, did you consider that if you find the person who killed Vivienne, they might decide to act against you?"

"Like what?" I asked. I tried to laugh, but it fell flat. "Kill me."

"Whoever killed her, they're ruthless and determined, and they're not going to play nice if you show up and start asking questions they don't like."

"I don't understand. First, I tell you I'm going to talk to the lawyer about this weird inheritance, and you jump straight to—" I blamed the gimlets, because it didn't land until right then. "Wait, you think Mr. Huggins killed her?"

"I didn't say that."

"You think he's involved, though. You think that's how this happened."

"I think," Deputy Bobby said as he parked the Jeep in front of the house, "you should have your lawyer contact Mr. Huggins and let the two of them sort out the estate and inheritance. That's a perfectly rational thing to do. It's also, in this case, the safe thing to do."

The drizzle had stopped. The wipers stuttered once over dry glass, and Deputy Bobby turned them off. Then he killed the engine. The headlights went dark, and all of a sudden it was just the two of us in the Jeep, with the sound of the waves and the sound of branches heavy with water moving in the wind and the sound of his breathing.

"Go inside," he said, passing me my keys, "and get some sleep."

I thought I should say something, but I didn't know what, so I said, "Thanks for the ride."

"You need to leave this alone. For your own safety. Do you hear me?"

"Yes."

Exasperation made his voice pitchy. "What does that mean?"

"It means I heard you."

"But you're not going to stop. You're going to keep doing whatever you want."

Breakers threw themselves against the sea cliffs.

"All right," he said, unbuckling himself. He got out of the Jeep. "I tried."

"I'm sorry."

"No, you're not."

"I'm sorry I upset you."

He shut the door. Hard.

I climbed out of the Jeep, and Deputy Bobby was already walking down the drive. "Come inside and wait for West."

He kept walking.

"There's no shoulder on that road. You can't walk into Hastings Rock."

But he didn't stop. And he didn't look back.

I stood there until I couldn't see him anymore. The keys bit into my hand. The wind cut through my T-shirt and shorts. Huddled against the cold, hugging myself, I told myself to go inside. My head was pounding again. I needed sleep. Lots and lots of sleep.

Who do you think you are? The question popped into my head too late, after Deputy Bobby had dissolved into the rain-swept night. What right do you have to tell me what to do, or what's safe, or how I should act when an entire town thinks I murdered their neighbor? How dare you act like that? And how dare you walk off? That's childish. It's worse than childish. We were having a conversation.

Go inside, I told myself. It's cold and wet out here, and he's gone, and what are you even doing?

But I didn't go inside. Instead, I walked around the house (it was a big house, and it was a long walk) until I reached the cliffs. I cleaned the mist from my glasses again. There was enough ambient light that the ocean looked like something sewn out of glitter, restlessly moving. I stared down, trying to remember where I'd seen Vivienne. I looked up to her room, to the balcony from where she had fallen. I looked back down again. I remembered the scarlet bobbing in the gray-green water. My face and arms were wet from the mist. Whatever had been roiling inside me, it drained out slowly, and then I only felt tired. I turned to go back into the house.

And then I saw it—a flash of white among the stunted hemlock that grew between the house and the cliff. I looked at it for what felt like a long time. I wiped the wetness from my face again. And then, picking a path carefully along the rocky edge, I pushed through the hemlock toward that white blaze. I stopped and stared.

It was a sneaker. Attached to a denim-clad leg. I turned on the flashlight on my phone, and it gave a pallid light that brushed back a little of the gloom. From deeper under the hemlock, Mr. Huggins stared back at me. He was dead. I started to step back, but something glinted in his hand, and I leaned closer for a better look.

It was a bracelet. And it was mine.

No indecision this time; I darted forward and plucked it from his hand, and then I scrambled to safety.

My bracelet. Mine. And it had been in his hand. If anyone else had found him—

I shut down that line of thought. But as I placed a call to 911, I couldn't stop the words from slipping out of my mouth: "You have got to be kidding me."

CHAPTER 9

A long night. A long, long, terrible night.

It went about like you'd expect. Deputies came. I was put in the back of a patrol car. More deputies came. A deputy took an initial statement. Even more deputies came. And then the sheriff came.

I kept my discovery of the bracelet to myself. I still wasn't ready to think about what that meant.

Deputy Bobby didn't come. In the intervals when I wasn't being questioned, I told myself it was because he was off duty. He probably didn't even know. And, of course, he wasn't really my friend—he was someone I knew, one of the few people I knew, and he'd been kind enough to give me a ride home.

I had to give my statement multiple times, and the sheriff had a lot of questions. I answered them as best I could, giving an accounting of my day, everything from when I'd woken up to when I'd found Mr. Huggins. I had witnesses who could place me at the library and at the Otter Slide, but I wasn't sure about the rest of the day. When the questioning became more intensive— when the sheriff wanted to take me to the station, when he wanted to talk about the inheritance—I asked if I was under arrest and said the magic word: *lawyer*. And then I did it again. And then again. And finally, after saying a lot of words you can't say on TV, the sheriff told me to get out of there because I made him sick, etc.

I checked my room for secret passages, moved my impromptu barricades into place, and fell asleep as soon as I hit the mattress.

When I woke, sunlight was streaming in through the window, and for a moment, I thought I was back home. It would be another bright, beautiful (hot) summer day in Providence. Hugo would already be up. He'd already have exercised. He'd already have done his writing. He'd have coffee for me, and he'd want to talk while I ate a Pop-Tart (okay, two—sue me). For a moment, it was all real. And I thought maybe I'd been wrong. I thought maybe I'd been happy.

Then reality came back to me in the form of a massive, canopied bed and what I thought might be a Chippendale tallboy pushed up against the bathroom door. Vivienne's murder. The scene with Pippi. That weird, ugly end to my conversation with Deputy Bobby. Poor Mr. Huggins. And then the hours of interrogation by the deputies and sheriff. A dull throbbing at the back of my head suggested I sleep for approximately another week, but somehow I got myself out of bed. I moved the furniture back into place. And then I got ready for the day.

After a shower and some vigorous toothbrushing (teethbrushing?), I felt marginally human again. I found a Fortnite tee with a provocative banana on it, and then—because Dashiell Dawson Dane eventually figures things out, no matter how stupid he may seem to the untrained eye—I checked the weather. The day was bright and sunny. Light sparkled on the waves. No rain, no clouds, no mist, no gloom. Definitely shorts weather. I added a pair of low-top Chucks. This was what I had imagined an Oregon summer would be like: perfection.

I made my way down to the kitchen, considering the possibility that, since Vivienne was no longer technically employing Indira, I might have to start fending for myself. (And honestly, the thought of messing up a batch of scrambled eggs was significantly less terrifying than Indira.) But when I got to the kitchen, there was a foil-wrapped plate on the counter with a sticky note that said DASH. Next to it, I found a jar of preserves that—oh my God. They were huckleberry. I removed the foil and found a stack of johnnycakes. Buttered johnnycakes. Buttered, golden, perfectly crispy and soft johnnycakes. And they were still somehow, miraculously, warm.

I devoured them. And the huckleberry preserves. And a couple of glasses of milk from the fridge. And a *lot* of coffee. At the kitchen counter, yes, because sitting down would have meant taking a break from stuffing my cornhole with johnnycakes.

I wasn't sure when Keme got there; he just seemed to be there all of a sudden, standing in the doorway to the servants' dining room. He was barefoot, in board shorts, and vanishing inside a Quiksilver hoodie. His long dark hair was pulled back, and it exposed the lines of his face, making him look older.

"Uh, hi." I wiped huckleberry jam from the corner of my mouth. "Sorry. I know there's probably some lion-meets-wildebeest energy going on right now, but I was starving—"

He turned and left. A few moments later, voices picked up in the distance, and then, to my surprise, laughter.

I followed the sound into the servants' dining room. Nobody was there, but the door to the cellar stood open, and a fresh wave of laughter floated up. Indira, Fox, and Millie. I hesitated a moment at the threshold. They wouldn't want to talk to me, not now. One murder, they could politely look the other way, but two…

But the reality was that I needed to talk to them. I needed to know if anyone had seen anything strange around Hemlock House the day before. (For example, it would be ideal if someone had seen Mr. Huggins getting murdered.) And I wanted to know if they'd ever heard Vivienne talk about changing her will, or well, how I might suddenly be the owner of what had to be millions of dollars' worth of property.

The steps down to the cellar were narrow, and the treads looked like they'd been cut by hand. The finished plaster gave way to a stone foundation, and the air took on familiar scents of sunless places and chill earth, in a way that made me think of turning over a rock in spring or, maybe more aptly, a cave. When I reached the bottom, I took in my surroundings: the room wasn't large, and there was no suggestion that the cellar was like a modern basement. It was small, and it clearly had been intended for function: storing fruits and vegetables, I guessed, when the house had first been built. Old wooden shelves stood in rows, with narrow aisles between them, and they were lined with jars of pickles and bags of dried peas and what looked like canned chicken from Costco.

"DASH!"

A supersonic hug (with a tiny human behind it) collided with me a moment later.

"Oh my God, are you okay? He's okay, everyone. You are okay, aren't you? We were so worried!"

They didn't look particularly worried. Indira was transferring jars of preserves from a basket between her feet to the shelves. Keme perched on a wooden box, glowering at me. And Fox lay on the ground, arms and legs akimbo.

"I'm fine," I said. "A little tired; it was another long night."

"We should just run away," Fox moaned. "We should start new lives in Mexico."

"They're having a crisis of artistic vision," Indira told us.

"I'll never make anything beautiful again. It's over. It never even began. I've spent my entire life bilking people out of their money for junk. Why isn't there any cake in this basement?"

"Did you eat?" Indira asked. "I left something for you."

There was something in the tone, and Millie looked at Keme, and the two of them burst out laughing. I had a sneaking suspicion that I knew what they'd been laughing about before I came down here.

"I did," I said, and I surprised myself with a grin. "The johnnycakes were delicious. Keme saw—it wasn't my cutest moment."

The amusement on Keme's face died, and he scowled at me again. It was so different from how he looked at everyone else. The boy didn't talk much (I'd never heard him say a word), but the longer I spent around him, the more I realized how expressive his face was. I'd seen chagrin and annoyance and comfort on his face, at different moments, when Indira talked. When Fox spoke, there was usually an underlying current of amusement. And I would have had to be blind to miss how he felt about Millie. But for me (unless he was laughing) there was only this…well, the best word was hostility.

"Keme, I'm sorry if we got off on the wrong foot. I feel like I might have offended you or upset you somehow. I really am sorry—if there's some way I can make it right, I hope you'll let me know."

I got nothing in return but the glare.

After a moment, Indira sighed and reached over to smooth down Keme's hair. He yanked his head away and turned the look on her.

"Don't give me that," Indira said in a quiet voice. "We talked about this."

The contest of wills lasted a few heartbeats. Keme broke first, looking down at the floor. When he brought his eyes up, he gave me a mocking smile and threw a shaka. Indira sighed again, but she went back to working on the preserves.

"Cool," I said and threw a pretty weak shaka of my own. It only made Keme roll his eyes and look away, but some of the charge in the moment seemed to have faded.

"Fox," Indira said, "get up or I'm going to step on you."

"I deserve to be stepped on. I'm nothing but life's welcome mat, with a million different tourists wiping their feet on me."

"I'll help you up," Millie offered.

"Thank God," Fox said. "There's a good girl."

As Millie got Fox upright, Indira said, "I ought to make you and Keme put these away."

"I have no idea what you're talking about," Fox said, although the injured dignity of the comment was weakened, somewhat, by the fact that they were stealing a Snickers from a box of assorted candy bars.

"Don't think I haven't noticed food going missing," Indira said, looking over her shoulder first at Fox and then at Keme. "If you want something, just ask."

Keme widened his eyes; his face was full of an outrage that, for a moment, made him look like a child again. I'd seen that look on the faces of some of the eighteen-year-olds I'd taught.

Indira, though, was unfazed. "I'm serious. Fox, one Snickers; don't take anything else."

"I was looking at it," Fox said, letting a Butterfingers slither back into the box. When Indira wasn't looking, though, they grabbed the Butterfingers again and tossed it to Keme. The boy caught it and made it disappear inside the hoodie.

Indira, with her back to them, just sighed and shook her head. Millie was trying to hide a smile.

"Oh," I said, "speaking of things going missing. I don't suppose you know who has keys to Hemlock House?"

Indira gave me a quick, assessing look. "As far as I know, Vivienne was the only one with a complete set. But the sheriff took her keys. I have a key to the back door—it works on the side door as well, I suppose, although I don't come in that way often. And I have keys to the coach house. Why?"

"I guess it doesn't really matter, but I think somebody went through my stuff. Again, I mean. After the deputies finished their search. But since I don't have a key, I've been leaving the house unlocked, so somebody could have come inside whenever they wanted."

Indira traded a look with Fox, and when she spoke, she sounded troubled, "I haven't seen anyone, Dash. I certainly wouldn't have let someone wander through the house."

"Maybe it was the deputies again."

"I didn't see any deputies."

"Maybe they came while you were in the coach house. Or if you went for a walk or something."

"Maybe," Indira said, but she didn't sound convinced.

"Maybe it's a GHOST!" Millie said.

In the midst of unwrapping their Snickers, Fox winced. "There's no such thing as ghosts."

"I saw a ghost once," Millie said. "At the shipwreck!"

Fox didn't argue, but their face said what they thought of the story.

"And Hemlock House has lots of ghosts. There's Swingin' Susan, and there's the Bird Man, and Princess Margaret—" She was ticking them off on her fingers and then her face lit up. "Oh! And Adolpha the She-Wolf!"

"That seems like a lot of—" I began.

"Of course, silly. To guard the treasure. There's Black Bart and the Mutineer and Lord Livingstone in Chains."

She was close to running out of fingers, so I tried again, "How can one house have—"

"Oscar, the one in the hunting accident, and Oscar Two, he's the one who got his head bashed in after he stole a dinghy, and the Daughters of the Sea. And—"

Keme made an annoyed noise. Fox rolled their eyes.

"The best one of all, Emmeline Grace, the Walking Widow."

"Don't most widows walk?" I asked.

"Yes, but she MOANS while she walks." Millie's words had gale-force excitement. "You can see her on the widow's walk at night sometimes."

Millie was clearly waiting for some kind of reaction, so I said, "Oh. Cool."

Keme made sure I saw him roll his eyes.

"No more talk about ghosts," Indira said. "Dash has dealt with enough death lately." She gave me another considering look. "Are you sure you're okay?"

"I honestly don't know. I'm functioning. I guess the complete nervous breakdown comes later."

"You're not going to have a breakdown," Fox said. "I'm going to have a breakdown because I've lived my entire life leaning on the crutch of my artistic genius, and now my world is crumbling."

"It's not all bad," Millie said. "I mean, I'm sorry for poor Mr. Huggins and, of course, for Vivienne. But Dash owns Hemlock House now! That means we can all stay and nothing has to change!"

The information clearly wasn't news—I guessed that Millie had told them about Pippi's revelation as soon as she got here, although it was possible they'd heard it from someone else in town. But the rest of Millie's statement caught me off guard. I hadn't considered how their lives would change after Vivienne's death. Indira would have to find a new job and a new home. Fox would be at the mercy of the new owner to complete their artistic project (I wanted to say it was something with wallpaper, but that conversation seemed eons ago). If Indira moved far away, Keme would lose the one person he seemed truly connected to. And Millie—well, Millie would be fine (she'd listed a large family, as I recalled), but she'd lose her friends.

"I think it's a bit more complicated than that," Indira said gently.

"It's a mare's nest," Fox said. "And we don't even know if he really owns the place. Do you?"

I shrugged. "I have no idea. I don't know how it could be possible. It's not like I bought the place—I would have remembered that, trust me."

Indira and Fox shared another of those looks. Indira spoke first. "Did Vivienne say anything about it?"

"Nothing. I started thinking that maybe I'd gotten some papers mixed up—she told me there was a fair amount of paperwork before I could start my job—but then I realized I never signed anything. We were going to sign the paperwork when Mr. Huggins showed up, and then I didn't see Vivienne again until—" I stopped myself, but the unsaid words hung in the air.

"She never said anything to me about her will," Indira said. "Or about Hemlock House. I don't mean to offend you, Dash, but I didn't get the impression that she knew you well or had any particular fondness for you. When she mentioned you, it all seemed professional."

"No, that makes sense. We didn't know each other."

Fox chewed slowly. "A beneficiary deed, maybe. The property transfers to you upon her death, and it doesn't have to go through probate like the rest of the estate. Although having it processed by the recorder of deeds—well, that seems like a snappy turnaround."

I tried to choose my words carefully. "I got the impression from the deputies—"

"You mean Bobby," Millie said. "Indira saw him drive you home last night."

Heat rushed into my face.

"And we decided you two are super cute together. Well, Fox and I decided."

"He has a boyfriend," I said.

"That's what Indira said, but Fox said—"

"What did Deputy Mai tell you?" Indira asked.

"Uh, I mean, he didn't tell me, but he kind of suggested that if the will and the deed had been manipulated, the most likely person would have been Mr. Huggins."

"That makes sense, in a weird way," Fox said. "Use the will and the deed to misdirect. Everyone is looking at you, assuming you killed Vivienne because she made you her heir."

"Pippi's version of events."

"Meanwhile, Mr. Huggins gets away with murder and with stealing all of Vivienne's money."

"Wait, what?"

"Vivienne was broke." With exaggerated innocence, Fox asked, "I didn't mention that?"

"Fox," Indira said, and she sounded like my mom when she was losing her patience.

"Tell us, tell us, tell us," Millie said.

Keme even leaned forward on the box, clearly ready to capture every word.

"It took some time actually going through Vivienne's records because she's been shuffling money from one account to another—trying to keep all the balls in the air, I guess, and paying these bills with that money while she waits for royalties to show up in that account. That kind of thing. So, there are a lot of transfers, a lot of fluctuating balances. But she's broke. She's got nothing. I mean, she was barely paying her bills."

"That doesn't make any sense," I said. "She has to have tons of money. The TV show, the books, all those real-life cases she helped solve."

"But she doesn't," Fox said. "It's gone."

"Mr. Huggins stole it," Indira said thoughtfully.

"Well, that's an assumption. But somebody stole it, and I think Mr. Huggins might have done it."

"I never liked him," Millie said. "He cornered me in the dining room one time, and his breath smelled like liver."

Keme sat bolt upright on the box, his whole body stiffening.

"He and Vivienne had an argument, I think." I tried to think back to that night. "They were in her study all day, remember? And I woke up that night when Mr. Huggins left. He slammed the door. You know how you can just tell someone's angry?"

"HE KILLED VIVIENNE!"

After we'd all recovered from the flash-bang effect of Millie's pronouncement, I said, "I don't know. If he did, I don't know how we could prove it—remember, Vivienne's study was locked from the inside, and the only way in or out was through my bedroom."

"The only way that we know of," Indira said. "Couldn't there be another secret passage? Or—wait. Maybe Mr. Huggins lowered himself from the sleeping porch—it extends off of Vivienne's study. He crawled down, and then he came inside quietly, and then he left again, this time slamming the door so that you'd be sure to hear him leave."

Millie's face was alive with excitement. "Or a NINJA! A ninja could have gotten into Vivienne's bedroom through the sleeping porch, and then he'd leave again the same way, and nobody would ever know."

"Not unless they happened to randomly guess a ninja," Fox said drily.

I opened my mouth—the explanations didn't feel right, for a few simple reasons: first, climbing up and down from the sleeping porch was clearly beyond Mr. Huggins's physical capabilities; second, the sheriff had said all the doors were locked, and I assumed that included the door to the sleeping porch; and three, I was (almost) a hundred percent certain zero ninjas were involved in this murder.

Before I could voice any of that, though, I caught a look at Keme's face: the transparent frustration on it, the hint of—well, I wanted to call it panic. He was shifting restlessly on the box, rubbing his hands on his knees.

"You thought of something," I said.

For an instant, he looked at me with gratitude. Then he held up two fingers.

"Two?" Indira said. "There were two people—"

"TWO MURDERS!" Millie sprinted across the cellar to squeeze Keme in a hug. "He's right! Mr. Huggins got murdered too!"

Which, yes, was a very good point, and one that we'd apparently all lost track of after the revelation about Vivienne's finances.

"Quite right," Fox murmured.

"Excellent point, Keme," Indira said.

"Okay," I said with a grin, "now I feel like an idiot. Thank God you're here."

To my surprise, Keme gave me a hesitant smile in answer. It folded almost immediately, but it had been there, and it had been real.

"So, what does that mean?" I asked. "I think we're on the right track—the sheriff's office seems to think so, too. I mean about Mr. Huggins and the money. There's definitely something suspicious there, and I didn't imagine that argument between Vivienne and Mr. Huggins before she died. But Keme's right. Someone killed both of them. Why?"

"To conceal their ill-gotten gain," Fox said. They were sidling toward the box of candy bars again, but they stopped when Indira gave them a look. "I think we're right to assume that Mr. Huggins was involved somehow. But let's be honest: we—" He indicated the four of them. "—knew Adrian Huggins, and that man's cheese, as the saying goes, done slid off his cracker."

I blinked.

"He wasn't very smart," Indira clarified. "I can't imagine he was a very good lawyer, and I have no idea why Vivienne used him—and apparently trusted him—for all these years."

"Because she liked people she could boss around," Millie said. Then she gasped and covered her mouth. Through her fingers she mumbled, "I didn't mean to say that."

"What do you mean?"

"No, I shouldn't have said that! Ms. Carver was so nice to give me a job!"

But Fox was giving Millie a strangely assessing look, as though they were seeing her for the first time. "No, that's right. Vivienne liked being the one with the upper hand in a relationship. She certainly did with Mr. Huggins; he jumped when she said jump—even if it was straight off a cliff." Fox grimaced. "God, that's not what I meant."

Indira ran fingers through her hair; that witch-streak of white caught the light. In a strained voice, she said, "She liked that I was reliant on her. She never said it, but I could tell. It came out in little ways."

I thought I could see the edges of what they were describing. Fox, with their dreams and visions and despair; Indira with her need for a home; Millie, who only wanted to be taken seriously; and me. I fit the pattern too. I needed work. I needed help. I would have been another baby bird in Vivienne's nest. Was that why she had been so quick to hire me? Because she knew I needed her more than she needed me?

I tried to bring my thoughts back to the conversation. "You think Mr. Huggins helped someone else steal the money?"

Fox spread their hands. "I think somebody has that money. Whether Mr. Huggins had a partner in crime or he was a patsy or he was simply someone's tool, well, that's harder to tell."

"It might not be the money." Indira had mussed her hair without seeming to realize it, and it gave the witchy vibes an extra spark. "It might be hate. Or love. Someone who needed Vivienne the way we all did. Someone who hated needing her. And hated Mr. Huggins too."

"What about Pippi?" I asked. "What about that manuscript?"

No one seemed to know what to say to that.

After a moment, Fox said, "What I wouldn't give to see Mr. Huggins's finances."

It took me a beat too long to realize what had happened. Millie was looking at me with untrammeled excitement. Indira was looking at me in sympathy. Keme was looking at me like he knew that somehow I was going to screw everything up. And Fox was looking at me like they meant to shove me out of a plane at ten thousand feet.

"Hold on a minute," I said. "Why does it have to be me?"

CHAPTER 10

The short answer, it seemed, was *because you're so good at it*, which was what Fox kept saying every time I objected.

Hours later, after waiting for the deputies to finish their search of Mr. Huggins's home, we were sitting in Fox's ancient van on a residential street in the eastern part of Hastings Rock. The homes were a mixture of bungalows and cottages that had a battered, huddled look, and although the streets were clean and the yards were kept, the air was stagnant and full of bugs, and there was a faint, unpleasant odor that had seeped into the car slowly in spite of the closed windows. This part of town, Fox had informed me on the drive over, had marshy areas; the Swift River created the eastern border of Hastings Rock, and that, along with its estuary, meant a very different (i.e., less desirable for most people) geography than the coast to the west or the bluffs and sea cliffs to the south. All of which only begged the question: why had Mr. Huggins lived here?

"But I don't want to be good at it," I finally tried.

"Alas, you can't always get what you want."

"Did you combine The Rolling Stones with 'alas'?"

"Dashiell," Fox said, patting my shoulder as though, perhaps, this would distract me. "I understand that you don't feel comfortable—"

"Breaking and entering, no, I don't."

They raised their hands in surrender, but they continued, "And that's to your credit. But you do seem to have a knack for this—"

"So do you! You were great when we snuck into Vivienne's office!"

"And I already explained: I can't do it because I'm going to be the lookout. I'm the perfect lookout, you understand. People know me. They see me wandering around, doing strange things all the time. You are a suspected murderer and, on top of that, the new kid in town. You would stick out like a sore thumb. I, on the other hand, am a local artist. I'm so eccentric I'm practically invisible."

"It sounds like you rehearsed this. And I thought you weren't an artist. I thought you were a fraud and a sham and a huckster."

"That," Fox said—a little huffily in my opinion—"was earlier. And what would you do instead? Would you rather send Millie in there?"

I gave them a flat look.

"Exactly," Fox said. "Would you rather subject Indira to the threat of bodily harm in her, uh, advanced state?"

"Did you just call Indira old?"

"No, no, no!"

"You're basically the exact same age."

"Not really the point—"

"And Millie and Keme think I'm basically the same age as you because I'm past twenty-five."

"But if you—wait, really?" Fox settled back and blinked at me. "That's depressing."

"It's depressing for you?" I asked.

"Who do they think is cooler? Wait, do they still say cool?"

"I'm getting out of the car now. Please pay attention and don't let anyone murder me."

"A gentle maiming at the very most," Fox promised me, holding out a pair of disposable gloves.

Somehow, I managed not to slam the door.

Mr. Huggins's house was a small Cape Cod that blended in with the other houses on the street. It had asbestos-shingle siding in a utilitarian brown, and the curtains were drawn in all the windows. Fox had parked on a side street, so I approached the house from the back rather than the front door. Privacy hedges screened the backyard (perfect for the discerning murderer lying in wait), and with only a distant streetlight for illumination, it took me a moment to find the gate in the gloom. I pulled on the disposable gloves and let myself into Mr. Huggins's backyard.

It was much darker back here, with the hedges blocking the light from the street. From what I could make out, the yard was as utilitarian as the house— the grass was cut, but there were no flowerbeds, no rosebushes, nothing that indicated Mr. Huggins had taken an interest in this part of his property. A darker shadow suggested a shed at the back of the lot, but I decided to leave that for later; I had a mental vision of opening it and a body falling out, probably landing directly on me, and I just wasn't emotionally equipped to handle that.

A few steps brought me up to the Cape Cod's back porch. I reached for the door, and then I stopped. I hadn't thought about this part. I had a sneaking suspicion that Fox had, and that Fox had conveniently forgotten to mention it. How was I supposed to get into a locked and sealed house? Police tape crisscrossed the back door, daring me to try. Maybe a window? Or—

And then I noticed that the door wasn't fully shut. Something seemed strange, and when I leaned down to check, I saw that the door and jamb were splintered near the strike plate. Which meant, my seasoned crime junkie brain told me, that someone had forced their way into Mr. Huggins's house. Why? Who? The deputies? Maybe they'd felt like they couldn't wait for a locksmith. Or maybe it had happened before the deputies got here. Or maybe, I thought with a frisson, it had happened after. Because someone had been waiting for the deputies to leave. The same way I had.

I thought about going back to the car. I thought about calling it a night. But—but what would happen next? Because the problem was, I was sure something was going to happen next. The killer, whoever it was, was determined to frame me. Vivienne's will. Hemlock House. Even that stupid secret passage in my bedroom, although I had no idea how they'd arranged that. And then my bracelet on Mr. Huggins's body. Someone was determined to make me take the fall for these killings, and if I went back to the car and told Fox to take me home, I'd just be sitting there, waiting for them to make the next move. And the next move would probably put me in a prison cell for the rest of my life.

When I prodded the door with one finger, it rocked open a few inches. The hinges didn't squeak. There wasn't a gust of suspiciously foul-smelling air. No ominous music began to play in the background. I wet my lips and gave the door another push, and it opened farther. The deputies had forced the door, I decided. Or someone else, someone who had come before the deputies got here. The killer, I thought. Wouldn't the killer have come over here straightaway? They wouldn't have waited for me to find Mr. Huggins's body.

It all sounded, to my own expert ear, like someone trying to rationalize while on the brink of a panic attack.

I forced myself to move. I squeezed between the strips of police tape and found myself in the kitchen—even in the dark, I could tell from the glowing clocks on the appliances. I turned on the flashlight on my phone and looked around. Walnut cabinets. Laminate countertops. The sink had some rusty-looking gunk congealed around the handles and the tap, and the vinyl tiles underfoot were peeling up in a million different places. Fingerprint powder covered pretty much everything. But what made me stop and stare was the detritus of smashed plates and bowls, the spilled coffee grounds and tea bags and what appeared to be Honeycomb cereal. The mess covered the floor, and I knew, in a heartbeat, the deputies hadn't done that. Someone had come through this house looking for something. And they'd been in a frenzy.

An opening on the far side of the kitchen connected with the living room. I picked a path through the destruction, wincing every time I jarred a piece of crockery, and the sound of ceramic grating against ceramic broke the silence. The living room didn't appear to be in much better condition. There was a Naugahyde recliner and a microsuede sofa, and the art prints of the Oregon Coast had the black poster frames you could get at Walmart. One thing was immediately clear to me: Mr. Huggins had never had a woman (or, for that matter a gay man) inside this house. Ever. One of the lamps looked like a lady's leg, complete with stocking and garter. I was pretty sure it was from a movie.

The destruction continued here. Cushions slashed. Drawers pulled out of tables and the entertainment center. A *CHiPs* VHS had been half unspooled, a glossy black snake of magnetic tape doubling back on itself on the floor. The lamp had somehow survived unscathed; maybe someone's artistic sensibilities hadn't permitted wanton destruction.

The front door was still locked (I checked), and a flight of stairs led to the Cape Cod's second floor. Instead of going up, though, I circled back to the kitchen and followed a short hallway past a small laundry room (torn apart), a powder room (the toilet lid lay on the floor in two pieces), and then the master bedroom (ransacked). Clothes lay everywhere. Photos had been ripped from the frames. The box spring and mattress had been leaned against the dresser and then slashed open. The attached bathroom had suffered even worse, with drawers staved in and the mirror shattered. They'd been getting angrier. They hadn't found what they were looking for.

What were they looking for? And for that matter, what was I looking for? I wasn't sure. Anything that explained why Mr. Huggins might have tried to frame me for Vivienne's murder. Or who his accomplice—or employer—might be. Anything, basically, that might help me make sense of the events of the last few days. Admittedly, that was a pretty wide net to cast, and as I stared at the savagery of the search that had been conducted here, I felt dismay and, yes, a little panic growing inside me. There was no way I had time to search through this chaos. And, worse, I had a feeling that if there'd been anything to find, it was gone now.

But giving up now meant going back and waiting for the killer to come after me again, so I looped back to the front of the house and went upstairs. The treads creaked quietly underfoot, but the rest of the house felt still. The air seemed mustier; it smelled like carpet that needed to be replaced, with a hint of something my brain associated with foot powder. When I got to the small landing at the top, I had three doors to choose from; all three stood open. The one to my right looked in on what had probably been a guest room before someone had torn it apart. The one directly ahead of me opened onto a small bathroom, which had also been searched. And to my left was Mr. Huggins's office.

The desk had been pulled out from the wall. Drawers had been ripped free and thrown to the floor. Banker's boxes lay on their sides, spilling papers everywhere. Paperwork spilled from a filing cabinet's gaping drawers. Mr. Huggins's diplomas had been knocked from the wall and now looked out from behind shattered glass (an Oregon State man, and then University of Oregon for law school). No computer, although cables suggested that there had been one until recently. Either the killer had taken it, or the deputies had.

Crouching, I took a closer look at the papers strewn across the floor. I wasn't a lawyer, but I recognized legalese and boilerplate, and there was plenty of both. A lot, actually. And although occasionally I saw another name, it looked like much of the paperwork was Vivienne's—contracts with publishers, licensing agreements, even banking and investment documents. That slowed me for a moment. I wondered if that was normal. Did lawyers often handle that kind of financial work for their clients? I had no idea. My mom and dad had a number of people who helped with financial issues, but most of it went through their accountant, not their lawyer. So, why had Mr. Huggins had this stuff? I thought about the will that Mr. Huggins had somehow faked. I thought about the deed he had somehow forged. I thought about what Fox had said, about Vivienne's finances. She'd been broke. And that just didn't make any sense. Not unless Mr. Huggins had been stealing from her.

I gathered some of the paperwork to take a closer look. Mr. Huggins's chair lay on the floor, its cushion slashed, so I moved over to the dormer window, with its built-in seat. Diffuse light from the street filtered through the thin curtain, pushing back the darkness a little, but I'd need my phone to read—

As I sat, the seat gave slightly beneath me. And I instantly knew what it was: the lid for the window seat's storage compartment. I stood and considered the seat again. It was just painted wood, and now that I was looking for it, I could see where the top of the bench was cut to allow for the storage compartment's lid to open and close. But from a distance, if you were in a hurry, it might have looked solid.

I dropped the papers I'd gathered, knelt, and opened the window seat. The storage compartment was a decent size, and inside was another banker's box. An untouched banker's box. One box. Only one.

Inside were files. Lots of files. Old files, to judge by the smell of aging paper and mildew. I took one out, flipped through it, and stopped. I went back to the beginning and looked at each document more closely. The paperwork all had to do with the Matrika Nightingale case. And it didn't look like newspaper clippings. It looked like official paperwork. The stuff that police investigations—and subsequent court cases—are made out of. And it was here. Inside Mr. Huggins's office. Hidden.

As I continued to scan the pages, something caught my eye, and I stopped. I went back and read the page again. It appeared to be the prosecutor's affidavit charging Matrika Nightingale with ORS 163.107, which I didn't have to be a genius to know must have meant murder in the first degree. But what made me stop and go back and make sure I wasn't imagining it was the prosecutor's name on the affidavit: Adrian Huggins.

I flipped to the next page mechanically, still trying to make sense of what I'd seen and why—how—Huggins could be connected to the Nightingale murders. But then I stopped thinking and stared at the page in front of me. It looked familiar, and I knew where I'd seen this kind of thing before: the loose-leaf paper, the furious ballpoint scribble, even the handwriting. The words scrawled across the page said *You set me up.* And there were more. Dozens and dozens of them. All neatly filed away in Mr. Huggins's secret box. Like Vivienne's own collection of messages from Matrika Nightingale.

My phone buzzed. I grabbed it by instinct and saw a message from a number I didn't recognize: *Somebone's coming.*

Another message came through: *Someone's coming.*

The sound of the back door opening was faint. I almost thought I'd imagined it. Then I heard footsteps.

I snapped a photo of the affidavit and Matrika's note, and then I lowered the lid on the window seat. I climbed onto it to check the window. It had ancient cam locks that were rusted shut, and no matter how hard I tried, they refused to turn. Maybe the dormer in the guest bedroom, I thought. Or the window in the bathroom. The footsteps were still moving slowly around the main floor.

As I hurried toward the landing, I told myself, Maybe it's just a deputy. Maybe someone saw my flashlight, and I'm going to get chewed out and arrested and thrown in jail, which all sounded preferable to being trapped inside a '90s-era bachelor pad with a frustrated murderer.

Before I could step out of the office, though, a voice came from downstairs.

"What are you doing here?" Sheriff Jakes asked.

For a moment, I thought he meant me. And then I realized the voice had come from too far away, and he must have been speaking to someone else.

A gunshot clapped through the house. Someone shouted. Footsteps rang out. And then another gunshot cracked the air.

I was moving before I could consider what I was doing. I sprinted down the stairs, swung around the newel at the bottom, and stumbled through the debris in the living room. Then I stopped.

Sheriff Jakes lay on the floor, and he wasn't moving. Standing over him was a woman. It took me a moment to place her—in part because she was older than she'd been in the pictures, and in part because of the clothes: a baggy cardigan, mom jeans, a black paisley bandana over her hair: Matrika Nightingale.

It didn't seem possible, but there she was. She had pouches under her eyes, a hint of a double chin, and a pallor that, even in cloudy Oregon, suggested a need for industrial quantities of Vitamin D. Something about her seemed familiar, and then I realized where I'd seen her before: the woman at Pippi's author reading, the one in a fedora and trench coat.

"I didn't do it," Matrika said, and that's when I noticed the gun in her hand. "I didn't do it!"

The front door flew open, and Deputy Bobby charged into the room. A moment later, the back door flew open, and the female deputy I remembered from Hemlock House charged into the kitchen.

"Drop the gun!" Deputy Bobby shouted. "Drop the gun! Drop the gun!"

Matrika let the gun fall from her hand. She burst into tears.

And just like that, it was over.

CHAPTER 11

The questioning, believe it or not, didn't last all that long. After Matrika had been handcuffed and taken away, Deputy Bobby led me out to his cruiser. He held the door for me (passenger seat, not the back), and it reminded me of the other rides he had given me. And how he'd said, *You're kind of a smart aleck.* And the way moonlight had dappled his face as we drove through the spruce forest. I didn't feel much like a smart aleck right then, though, and the only light came from the soft glow of the dash and, far off, the old streetlamp down the block.

Deputy Bobby got behind the wheel. He rubbed his eyes. And then, voice strained, he said, "What were you doing?"

I told him.

After I'd finished, he didn't say anything for what felt like a long time. An ambulance came, and paramedics rushed into the house. Other sheriff's office vehicles began to arrive—lights on, but no sirens. A van marked MEDICAL EXAMINER was next. It made me think of that day in the kitchen when I'd thought I was so smart. I'd made that comment about a medical examiner removing Vivienne's body. The sheriff had taken the chance to put me in my place and told me he had the authority to remove it. I looked at the van and thought, But I guess the sheriff's dead now.

"Let me sort things out," Deputy Bobby finally said in that same wrapped-too-tight voice. "And I'll drive you home."

Through the windshield, I watched him as he moved from one deputy to another, answering questions, shaking his head. The scene wasn't exactly chaos—they were too well trained for that—but an electric current ran through everything like they were all about to jump out of their boots. Somewhere, a chief deputy was getting roused out of bed to learn two awful pieces of bad news: first, that the sheriff was gone; and second, that they were in charge now.

It wasn't long before Deputy Bobby came back. He buckled himself in, and we eased away from the house.

"Shouldn't you take me to jail?" I asked. I felt like I was floating, and like the words I was saying were drifting behind me as we drove. "Shouldn't you arrest me?"

"Do you want to be arrested?"

I shook my head.

He must have caught the movement in the darkness because he said, "Okay, then."

The trees. The smell of fir and salt and silty clay loam. The moon-shadows sweeping slowly back and forth.

Some of that floatiness started to go away, and I roused myself in my seat. "It doesn't make any sense."

Deputy Bobby stared out the windshield.

"None of it makes any sense."

"You've had a hard night. Take it easy."

A hard night didn't even come close, but that wasn't really the point. My brain was waking up again, and I couldn't make the pieces of the puzzle fit. "Did you know Matrika Nightingale had escaped from prison?"

"We knew. The penitentiary hadn't announced it publicly yet because they were hoping to bring her in before anyone found out."

"And you didn't tell me?"

That made him glance over at me. "No. I don't talk about ongoing investigations. That's policy."

Maybe, I thought, but that hadn't kept him from talking to me about the case when—well, when he'd been nicer to me. Before he'd turned into this Deputy Bobby, the one who seemed determined to be a hardnose about everything.

"Was she a suspect?" I asked.

It felt like a long time before Deputy Bobby said, "She was a consideration."

"A serial killer who escaped from prison, after she'd been threatening for years to kill the woman who put her in jail and the attorney who prosecuted the case—she was a consideration?"

"Wait, what?"

"She wasn't your prime suspect?"

"What do you mean the prosecuting attorney?"

"Mr. Huggins. He was the prosecuting attorney on Matrika's case. Nobody knew that?"

"How in the world was I supposed to know that? He was some two-bit lawyer who worked out of his house for a—" He managed to stop himself, but I had the feeling that whatever he'd been about to say, it wouldn't have been flattering to Vivienne. "We found out about Nightingale's escape after the investigation began." Deputy Bobby shifted in his seat. "And there was that secret passage from your room."

I rubbed my eyes. They itched with fatigue; everything from the last few days was catching up to me now that my adrenaline had peaked. "I cannot believe you didn't tell me." Before Deputy Bobby had to respond to that, I continued, "Never mind. It still doesn't make any sense. Let's say Matrika did kill Vivienne. Fine. But how did she get inside her room?"

"Maybe Vivienne let her in."

"The serial killer she put in prison?"

"Maybe Nightingale had a gun."

"Fine. She forces her way into the office with a gun, but instead of shooting Vivienne, she forces her out onto the balcony and pushes her."

"No noise," Deputy Bobby said. "She didn't want to wake anyone up."

"But what about Mr. Huggins?"

"Like you said, he was the prosecuting attorney."

"No, I mean the rest of it. Me inheriting everything. The deed to Hemlock House. That was all meant to frame me, and the only person who could have done it was Mr. Huggins. Why would he help Matrika murder Vivienne and frame me?"

"She threatened him. He was afraid for his life—reasonably, it turned out, since she killed him anyway."

"At Hemlock House?"

"She might have lured him there."

Everything Deputy Bobby said was—well, I wouldn't have said it made sense, but I could follow the chain of logic. The problem, though, was that it felt wrong. I didn't believe Matrika had frightened Mr. Huggins into framing me and then turned around, killed him, and tried to frame me again by leaving his body at Hemlock House with one of my bracelets on his body. It was too complicated, for one thing. And for another, Matrika didn't even know who I was—how could she have planned any of this to include me? But when I tried to organize my arguments, it was like trying to hold sand.

"Why come back? Why kill the sheriff?" Why, I almost added, did I believe her when she said she didn't do it?

Deputy Bobby's silence was broken only by the thrum of the tires. When he spoke, he sounded strangely defensive. "It was bad luck. She wanted something in that house—you saw how it was torn apart—and the sheriff walked in on her. You're lucky she didn't find you first."

I ignored the jab. I tried to replay the night's events. I was almost certain that I'd heard the sheriff moving around inside the house, and then the sound of a door, and then the sheriff asking, *What are you doing here?* Not like he was surprised—more like he was annoyed. What did that mean? Had he been working with Matrika? Had he been her accomplice this whole time?

"I don't know," I finally said. "It doesn't make any sense."

"It doesn't have to make any sense to you. That's the whole reason we have law enforcement officers." Deputy Bobby's voice softened fractionally as he added, "You need to get some rest. It's over; you don't have to worry about it anymore."

We finished our drive to Hemlock House in silence.

"Do you want me to come inside?" Deputy Bobby asked as he stopped at the door.

I shook my head and unbuckled my seat belt.

"I'm sorry for my tone earlier. It's been a stressful few days."

"Sure."

"I'm still trying to wrap my head around what happened. The sheriff, I mean."

I drew a breath and said, "I know. It's okay. I'm sorry I made things harder for you than they needed to be."

In the dark, with only the glow of the dash for light, I couldn't see the rich, burnished bronze of his eyes. They were just little slivers of light.

"Get some rest," he said again. "Are you sure you don't want me to come in?"

I nodded as I slid out of the cruiser. I shut the door, gave the car a little rap of goodbye, and headed inside.

Dark halls. Dark rooms. Big, dark silences. I got into my room and started to barricade the doors, and then I realized I didn't need to. They'd arrested Matrika. The case was closed. I lay in bed, staring up at the white ghost of the canopy. I wanted, with a visceral kind of pain, to go home. But the truth was that I didn't have a home. Not anymore. I wouldn't go back to Hugo. I wouldn't go home to my parents. I didn't belong here. I'd have to go somewhere else now. Start over. I'd have to figure out how to get a job. Maybe I'd move to Portland;

the joke I'd heard in Providence was that Portland was where young people went to retire.

Even though I felt wrung out, my eyes grainy, my head aching, sleep didn't come. And then my stomach rumbled.

Had I eaten dinner? I couldn't remember. Would Indira have left something to eat in the kitchen? If not, was I bold enough to try something myself? Maybe a peanut butter sandwich. Or I could DoorDash something. Or I could drive into town—a glance at the clock showed me it wasn't even eleven yet. I could go to the Otter Slide. I could have another delicious burger and fries.

Or you could check the kitchen, a voice said inside my head, and see if Indira left some of that cake.

No cake, I told myself. A peanut butter sandwich. A glass of—uh, warm milk? That was supposed to put people to bed. Detective Will Gower drank warm milk in one story. In that one, he'd been an Amish minister, though, and I'd been reading a lot of books about the Amish, and somehow warm milk had seemed like a crucially vivid detail for Brother Will.

Warm milk, I told myself as I padded downstairs. And one vegetable. My stomach roiled in protest, but I mustered my moral fortitude. A carrot, maybe. You could eat carrots if they were smothered in peanut butter.

The problem, though, was that Indira had left the cake right on the counter, and my moral fortitude went straight into the trash.

After a slice of cake and a glass of milk (cold, thank you), I felt a little better. I decided to forgive myself for the carrot slip-up. I would eat two carrots tomorrow. Or, better yet, I'd find somewhere I could get a smoothie. They could put as many carrots as they wanted in the smoothie as long as it tasted like banana-berry when they were done. I headed back upstairs. The only sound was the whisper of my steps on the rugs and, far off, the crash of waves. I thought maybe I'd try some reading. A comfort read. Maybe Sue Grafton.

I stopped in my doorway and forgot all about Sue because someone was rifling my suitcase. The figure was dressed all in black; they would have been invisible in the dark except for the flashlight they were holding. They must have heard me or sensed me, though, because they turned. For a moment, we were looking at each other—not that I could see anything with the flashlight shining in my eyes.

Too late, I managed to say, "Hey."

Will Gower would not have said *hey*.

I reached for my phone, and the figure broke into a run. They charged straight at me. In the dark, I had an impression of movement. The beam of the flashlight bobbed and strobed, making it hard to get a sense of space and distance. I tried to plant myself in the doorway, but I was too slow—I was off-balance when the figure crashed into me. They hit my shoulder, and I felt a big red warning light go on. I stumbled back, caught myself against the wainscotting, and managed to keep from falling. The figure in black, though, just kept running.

"Hey!"

It was a little better—at least this time it was a shout.

As soon as I had my feet under me, I took off after them. They charged down the grand staircase. I sprinted, almost slipped on a rug, and caught a baluster, which probably saved my life. My momentum spun me down the stairs—I kept myself upright somehow, but it felt like more of a controlled fall. And, somehow, I was gaining on the figure. The surprise, more than anything, had given them the advantage, and although running for exercise ranked high on my list of the seven deadly sins, I was definitely faster.

When the figure reached the bottom of the stairs, they darted left. That didn't make any sense; the front door was straight ahead. Instead, the figure darted into the den. The door slammed shut behind them. I barely heard the crash because my blood was pounding in my ears.

I reached the door a moment later. It was locked. I threw myself into it. That red light in my shoulder went on again. The door rocked in its frame. It was an old door, solid, not some hollow-core modern nonsense. But the latch was old too, and the house was old, and when I threw myself against the door the second time, the latch popped free of the frame. The door swung inward. I took in the room in a series of impressions: the dark paneling, the heavy curtains, the window, still shut, and the built-in bookshelves lining a cold fireplace. Gilt lettering on the spines of the books caught the faint ambient light like brushed gold.

Empty. The room was empty.

Somehow, they'd gotten away.

CHAPTER 12

"Hello?" Deputy Bobby's voice came from the vestibule, echoing through the stillness of Hemlock House. "Sheriff's Office. Mr. Dane?"

"In here," I called from the den. I was on my back, squirming around for a better look.

Footsteps moved toward me, and a moment later, Deputy Bobby said, "What in the world are you doing?"

"I'm trying to find the—uh, thief. Killer. Whoever it was."

"In the fireplace?"

I sat up. Carefully. I'd seen *Arrested Development* enough times (according to Hugo, way too many times) to know the dangers of sitting up quickly inside a fireplace. "They came in here, and they disappeared. Ergo, there's a secret passage. Ergo, I have to find it. Ergo, fireplace."

Deputy Bobby stood there for a while. Then he crossed the room, crouched, and looked me in the eye. "What are you on?"

"Three slices of cake and—how many cups of coffee are in a carafe?"

"That depends on the size of the carafe. And the size of the cup. And how much you brewed."

"I filled the water all the way to the top, ergo—"

"Okay," he said. "Let's get you out of there, and how about you try not to touch anything?"

"Why—" I took a look at myself, saw that I was covered in soot, and said, "Oh."

"Uh huh. Upsy-daisy."

He caught me under the arms and lifted, and somehow, I got to my feet without touching (and destroying) the priceless antiques around me. The possibility of a less-than-spotless fireplace hadn't occurred to me, but admittedly, I'd been in something of a frenzy after soothing myself with cake and coffee. Getting some sugar in my system—and caffeine—had seemed like the rational thing to do while waiting for a deputy to respond to my 911 call. In fact, it had been the only thing I could do; there had been a string of unanswered texts from Fox and Millie on my phone, but I couldn't deal with them right then. And now Deputy Bobby was here, and I was realizing in hindsight, of course it was exactly my luck that he would be the one who got the callout.

"Why are you here?" I asked him.

"Did you call 911?"

"I mean why you. I mean—I mean why you specifically. Not that I'm not happy to see you."

"Nice save."

"How would you like a hug?"

That goofy grin slipped out for a moment, and Deputy Bobby warded off my soot-stained embrace with one hand. "I happened to be the closest deputy when your call came in. Probably because everyone else is at Adrian Huggins's house, and I was still driving back after dropping you off."

"Oh."

"Want to tell me what happened?"

I did.

When I finished, Deputy Bobby said, "Stay here. I'm going to take a look around."

"Most of the cake had already been eaten. I need you to understand I wasn't starting with a full cake."

He looked at me for what felt like a long time before he sighed and left.

It wasn't long before he came back. "The house and the surrounding grounds are clear. Indira didn't hear or see anything." There was a strange note in his voice as he added, "Secret passages aside, the house appears to be empty."

"But you believe me, right?"

"I believe you." And then, without missing a beat, he added, "I don't agree with you, but I believe you."

"What does that mean?"

"It means we're going to stop looking for secret passages."

"What? Why? They came in here! And when I got the door open, they were gone."

"And the window isn't latched," Deputy Bobby said.

I opened my mouth. Then I stopped. Could they have gone out the window while I was trying to get the door open? Yes. Maybe. Possibly. And then slid it shut behind them. That seemed like an unnecessary step, but…maybe?

"Let's get you cleaned up," Deputy Bobby said. But when we left the den and I turned toward the kitchen, he said, "That's cute, but no." And he pointed to the stairs.

It wasn't until I got to the bathroom that I saw, well, the mess. I looked like that chimney sweep guy from *Mary Poppins*. I looked like that guy if he'd had a really bad day and possibly found a killer in his bedroom and then chased the killer through the house and—

The splash of water startled me. Deputy Bobby stood next to the clawfoot tub, trying to figure out the taps.

"Please tell me this place has hot water," he muttered.

"Get out of here," I said.

"I want you to lock the door behind me."

"I thought the house was empty."

"Both doors. And I don't need a smart aleck right now."

I gave him that jaunty little salute again.

He sighed. "Both doors."

"Both doors, Deputy Bobby."

"I'm going to see if I can lift any prints from the window. I don't know if I'll be able to do anything with your clothes or luggage."

"Aye-aye."

He sighed again when he stepped out of the room and pulled the door shut behind him. I pulled off my tee and hissed through my teeth as that red light went on in my shoulder again.

"You okay?"

"Fantastic."

A moment later, his voice carried clearly through the wood. "Why haven't I heard the lock yet?"

I locked the door.

"Both doors."

"Oh my actual God," I said. But I crossed to the other door and locked it too.

The hot water felt amazing. And there was something weirdly satisfying about seeing the soot snake off me and swirl around the drain. But mostly, it was just so...nice to have Deputy Bobby here. I suppose I should have felt terrified that someone had been in the house, that someone had risked going through my things while I was downstairs, that someone had disappeared as though by magic. Because I didn't buy the window explanation. And I had zero idea what someone would want from my belongings—unless they were planning to frame me yet again. Maybe the terror was there, waiting for me to be alone in the dark again. But right now, instead of feeling any of those things (except perpetually confused), I felt relaxed. Deputy Bobby was here. And he was being, well, kind. Again. Like the weird hardness of the last day had never happened.

Maybe because the water was warm, or maybe because of the way the spray kneaded sore muscles, maybe because I was experiencing a serious sugar crash, or maybe knowing that Deputy Bobby was there meant that, for the first time in days, I felt safe—whatever the reason, by the time I'd cleaned myself up, the water had sluiced away most of my coffee-and-cake-fueled buzz too. I slipped into a pair of sleep shorts and an ancient SEGA tee, and then, as I opened the bedroom door, I called out, "Deputy Bobby!"

Directly into his face.

Because he was, of course, standing right there.

Working a finger in his ear, he gave a mock grimace. "You've been spending too much time with Millie."

"I thought you were downstairs."

"What?"

"I thought—you jerk!"

The goofball smile flashed again. I stepped back to let him into the room. He looked at me, and I was suddenly aware of the sleep shorts, of the washed-to-transparency tee. I couldn't read what was in his face. Then he said, in a voice that was slightly different, "Had you never been to Oregon before?"

"What?"

"The shorts. The T-shirts. I mean, on a sunny day, sure. In August. But haven't you been freezing?"

"Uh, yes?"

"Was that a question?"

"Did you find anything on the window?"

The grimace was a real one this time, and he shook his head.

"Nothing?" I asked.

"Nothing usable."

"Great," I said. I flopped onto the bed and stared up at the canopy. "Perfect."

"I know this is hard to believe, but maybe it was a coincidence. We've got Matrika Nightingale in custody. And you've got to think about this from a different perspective. People will have heard about Vivienne's death. They know she was wealthy. They know about Hemlock House. And although Hastings Rock is cute and touristy, a lot of the coast isn't doing nearly so well. Someone probably thought it would be an easy score—walk into an empty house and take whatever they want."

I almost said, *From my suitcase?* But we'd already had a version of that argument.

The mattress dipped when he sat on the edge of the bed. The sense of safety and warmth I'd experienced was rapidly evaporating. Okay, the vanishing warmth was at least partly because Deputy Bobby was right (as usual), and I probably should have been wearing my flannel long johns. The chill damp of the sea had settled into everything, even the bedding. But in a few minutes, he'd leave, and I'd be alone again. And no matter what he said, I didn't believe the person in my room had been an opportunistic hooligan from a nearby town.

"Why are you here?"

The question—and how he said it, as though he'd reached the absolute pinnacle of bafflement—startled a laugh out of me. "Rude."

"You know what I mean." And then, his voice bent with what might have been amusement. "And sorry."

"I'm here because I thought I had this great job opportunity. Look how that turned out."

"No, you're not."

I stared up at the canopy. The roar of the waves seemed louder. Maybe someone had opened a window; that would explain the sound I heard rushing in my head.

"You're smart, obviously. I mean, you're definitely a smart aleck, but you're also very smart." Deputy Bobby paused as though trying to pick his next words more carefully. "And I'd like to say you have no sense of self-preservation, and possibly no common sense, but the truth is, you're brave, and you're determined, and you're capable. You could be anywhere. Doing anything. With anyone."

Why did that last part make me want to sit up and look into his face again, see if I could see it there again—whatever I'd seen when he'd looked at me a few moments ago, when I'd known he was looking at me?

Before I had to say anything, Deputy Bobby said, "I know what you told the sheriff. I know what you told Millie. I know you're a writer, and Vivienne's a writer, and on the surface it all makes sense. But your parents are famous writers."

I groaned. "You looked me up?"

"You were a murder suspect," he protested, but he laughed. "I had to do my due diligence."

This big house with all those big old clocks, and I couldn't hear a single one of them ticking.

"I'm sorry," he said. "It's none of my business."

"No, it's okay. It's a fair question. I'm embarrassed, that's all."

"You don't have to be embarrassed."

"That's easy for you to say since you don't know why I'm embarrassed." I tried to make the words light, but they fell flat anyway. I kept my gaze on the canopy, and I took slow, deep breaths as I talked. "I was in a relationship. His name was Hugo, and he was perfect. Everyone told me how perfect he was. My friends loved him. My parents loved him." I was still trying to breathe, but I felt like a giant's paw was wrapped around my chest, squeezing. Will Gower didn't cry, I thought as I blinked. Will Gower never cried. "And one day, I had to get out of there. I had to leave. I couldn't stay there one more day."

Deputy Bobby's silence was all saw-toothed edges, and when he finally spoke, his voice was ratcheted down. "If he hurt you, you can still—"

"No. God, no. He didn't hurt me. He didn't cheat on me. He didn't steal all my money. He told me he loved me." Maybe I imagined the sudden charge to the quiet in the room. Maybe it was only in my head. But even so, the hairs on my arms stood up, and goose bumps tightened my skin. "And I didn't love him. I told myself I did. Everyone else told me I did. Every single person I knew told me how perfect he was, and how lucky I was, and how we were a dream couple. And for a while, that was enough. And then it wasn't. So, I told him. And we broke up." I had to stop again. When I could, I said, "Hugo's a great guy, really. He's kind and patient and smart and funny. He's a much better writer than I am. And he loves me. But I'm not going to do that. Lie to him, I mean. Or lie to myself. I won't do it. So, that's why I'm embarrassed. Because it's such a small thing, and I was so dramatic about it—taking this job, moving across the country. There's no big horror story, just Dashiell Dawson Dane being a problem, as always." I tried to stop, but the words just kept coming. "See? Embarrassing."

Deputy Bobby's chest rose and fell with his breaths. That silent, electric charge intensified until I felt like my hair was going to pop off my head.

And then he said, "I don't think that's embarrassing. I think that's brave. I think *you're* brave."

Tears stung my eyes, and I had to swallow before I could speak. "My parents didn't think it was particularly brave. My dad told me I was being an idiot, and my mom asked if I would be uncomfortable if she still invited Hugo to Christmas."

A beat passed before Deputy Bobby said, "Jeez."

"It's okay. They just didn't know what to say. I don't think they were ever in love. They love their writing. They love talking to each other about their writing. I remember my mom was on a self-improvement kick and made a rule that we couldn't talk about work at the table—it lasted about two days, and those were the two worst dinners of my life. They just sat there. I honestly think they were on the brink of divorce, and it had only been two days." I shook my head. "I don't want that. I don't want to live like that."

He breathed. I breathed. And in the space between our breaths, I felt…something. Something trying to work its way out. Something fighting to be free.

"It was very brave," he said again, his voice low. "You should be proud of yourself."

It felt like more was coming, but he didn't say anything else. Finally, I said, "Thanks. I guess I'd feel prouder if I wasn't constantly questioning if I did the right thing. I mean, how are you supposed to know what love feels like? How is anyone supposed to know? Maybe I do love Hugo; sometimes I think I do. But most of the time, I think—I think if that's love, it's not enough. I want the kind of love that doesn't leave any room for doubt. But then I think, maybe that's a fantasy. Maybe what I feel for Hugo is all that anybody feels. Maybe everything else is just made up. Or maybe it's me. Maybe there's something broken in me, and maybe I'll never love anyone the way I want to. Maybe what I had with Hugo really was perfect—for me, I mean—and I threw it all away for a stupid dream." I had to fight to steady my voice, fight to sound joking when I added, "So, yeah, lots of overthinking and general indecisiveness."

Deputy Bobby turned, and I got a look at his face. The only word I had for it was raw, like his armor had been stripped away and I was seeing that naked, vulnerable part we all try to hide from the world. Then the armor came back. He was Deputy Bobby again—although a hint of it lingered in his eyes, pain or fear or plain old unsettlement. He started to say something and stopped. His throat moved. And then, his voice pleasantly raspy, he said, "You're not broken. And you're not wrong. You weren't indecisive. You made a decision—a hard one. And you shouldn't doubt yourself, not about this. You deserve that kind of love. And I think the world would be a better place if more people did what you did. If they were honest about their feelings. If they fought for what they wanted and didn't settle for less."

His eyes were that deep, polished bronze, and after a moment, I had to look away.

"You might possibly be broken in the head, though."

I gave him a glare.

"We haven't talked about your choice to creep downstairs after you heard a gunshot."

"It's what Will Gower would have done!"

"I have no idea who Will Gower is, but he sounds like he needs to be in a psych ward."

"Oh, one time he was, and his assistant—she was a match girl—" I managed to stop myself. I found a smile and dusted it off. "You stayed way longer than you should have."

Deputy Bobby shook his head.

"You did. You should have checked the place out and left. Tonight's got to be a disaster after—" I couldn't bring myself to say *the sheriff.* "I'm sorry I kept you."

"You didn't keep me. I was doing my job. And believe it or not, I would much rather spend time with you."

"I bet you say that to all the boys."

"No," he said. "I don't."

Something creaked in the house. Deputy Bobby sat up straight, hand going to the gun at his side. I shot up from the bed like I had a rocket strapped to me. But no other sounds came, and after a moment, I gave a shaky laugh. Deputy Bobby offered one of those wry smiles, but I noticed, in that moment before his hand relaxed, that his knuckles were white around his gun.

"What are you going to do now?" Deputy Bobby asked as he stood.

"I don't know. I guess go home? I mean, I didn't want to leave while I was still the prime suspect, but now that I'm not about to be arrested, I guess I'll go home and…figure things out. Whatever that means."

He was looking straight at me, his gaze direct and unwavering and unnervingly intense. And he said, "That would be a shame. Just one guy's opinion, but you definitely make things more interesting around here."

And I had no idea what to say to that.

The corner of his mouth turned, and he added, "But I meant tonight."

"Oh."

"Uh huh."

"Oh my God."

"That was a very dramatic pronouncement, though."

I covered my eyes. "Could you please step outside while I die of embarrassment?"

Even his laugh was nice. "Do you have someone who could stay with you? Or I could drive you to a motel—no, God, they're all full. I don't like the idea of you staying here alone."

I shrugged.

"If you don't mind staying up a few hours," Deputy Bobby said, and it took me a moment to identify the note in his voice as uncertainty, "You could stay with me and West—"

"WE'RE HERE!"

Millie's supersonic greeting boomed from downstairs.

Deputy Bobby's smile was funny. "Spoke too soon."

CHAPTER 13

Nothing I said could induce Deputy Bobby to stay. He had to get back to work. Which, the rational part of my brain acknowledged, was totally true and fair and appropriate. But I couldn't help feeling—disappointed? Was it disappointment when you felt a single moment of murderous intent toward the foursome who had tromped into your house and ruined—well, whatever that was?

We were in the kitchen, and Millie was still hugging me. Keme's face made it plain how he felt about that.

"We were so WORRIED!" she said for about the fourteenth time.

"We weren't that worried," Fox said. "Not after I saw that scrumptious Deputy Mai squire you away."

"He didn't squire me away," I said. "He was questioning me about a murder. Another one, I mean."

"Honey, listen to me: time alone with a delectable man is time alone with a delectable man."

"He has a boyfriend."

"This feels very objectifying," Indira said, "from someone who was lying on my kitchen floor not too long ago, moaning about the hypersexualization of the modern world."

"Yes," Fox said, "but have you seen Deputy Mai's tush?"

"And his face," Millie said, "he has the best face. Except for yours, Dash."

"Thank—"

"It's like two cantaloupes in compression shorts," Fox said. "Not yours, Dash. A bit flat, actually."

"—you. What is happening?"

"We're happy you're alive, dear," Indira said as she stirred something in a pot on the stove. Something hot. And chocolatey. And she had the mini marshmallows in a cute little bowl. "I see you enjoyed the cake."

"There was a cake-related emergency," I said. "I definitely didn't eat all that myself."

Keme snorted.

"What happened?" Millie asked. She finally released me. Keme was seated on a stool next to Indira, but I didn't miss the way he shifted in relief as Millie stepped away from me.

So, I told them about sneaking into Mr. Huggins's house, about how the door had already been forced, about how the place had been ransacked. I told them about the box of files on Matrika Nightingale that I'd found hidden in Mr. Huggins's office, about the revelation that Mr. Huggins had been the prosecuting attorney on the Matrika Nightingale case, and about what I'd heard downstairs: the sheriff's question, and then the gunshots.

Even as I was telling them, though, something about my own account seemed off. Yes, I'd heard the sheriff ask, *What are you doing here?* And there had been a gunshot. But had there been something else? Another shot, and then—a door? I'd heard a door slam, maybe. Possibly. But when? Before the gunshot? After? Was it a false memory? Witnesses were notorious for those.

"That doesn't make any sense," Fox said. "For Mr. Huggins to have been the prosecutor on the Nightingale case—well, he must have been a solid figure in the district attorney's office. Or a rising star, I suppose, but it seems hard to believe they'd have given a case that serious to anyone but an established professional. And Nightingale was convicted and sent to prison. That should have been a career-making case; how did he end up doing odd jobs for Vivienne in Hastings Rock?"

"Maybe he thought he'd get some of the same celebrity status as Vivienne," Millie said. "Maybe he thought they'd be a team, like they'd been on the Nightingale murders."

"But he didn't," Fox said. "Why? Why did he slink away and disappear?"

Indira came to the table with mugs of hot chocolate. When I took mine, that red light went on in my shoulder again, and I barely covered a wince. "What I don't understand," Indira said, "is why now?"

"What do you mean why now?" Millie asked. "She escaped. That's why."

"But why escape now? She's been in jail for decades—what has it been? Twenty years? Thirty? Has she really been obsessed with revenge for all that time?"

"Yes," Fox said, "obviously."

"Why wouldn't she run for the border? Disappear, start a new life? Why come here? And Dash made a very good point—why would Mr. Huggins help her?"

Millie and Fox both jumped in with answers, but the words washed over me in a swell of meaningless noise; I was just too tired. None of it made any sense. Something about Indira's question—why now?—tickled the back of my brain, but I couldn't form a coherent thought around the question. Because I'm here, I thought. Because apparently, I'm destined to get caught up in stuff like this.

I reached for the marshmallows (Indira's hot chocolate was amazing, of course, but she'd clearly miscalculated the correct number of marshmallows), and my shoulder lit up with pain again. Which really seemed a tad excessive for being bumped by a murderer-slash-burglar. I mean, I was young. I was in good shape. Decent shape. I did pushups. Well, I'd done one pushup. Once. Because Hugo had believed, in a truly endearing way, that I needed to get more exercise.

Movement made me turn, and I was surprised to see Keme standing next to me, an ice pack in his hand. He raised an eyebrow in question. I was still too surprised to really think about it, so I nodded. He wrapped a towel around the ice pack and pressed it to my shoulder.

Instant heaven.

Keme must have seen it on my face because he laughed, barely more than a breath, and adjusted the ice pack. Somehow, it was even better. It honestly felt so good that I thought, even with the cold, I could fall asleep—

"OH MY GOD!" The volume made it hard to tell Millie's tone, but I thought it was glee. "THEY'RE FRIENDS!"

Fox and Indira spun to look at us. In the wake of Millie's announcement, the silence was—to put it one way—deafening.

I looked at Keme. He didn't quite roll his eyes, but his face held a kind of reluctant amusement.

"Obviously we're friends," I said.

"Now you should get matching tattoos," Fox said.

This time, Keme did roll his eyes.

"Now you need to be BEST friends," Millie told us.

"One thing at a time," I said.

"You should be ROOMMATES!"

The kindest word for what must have shown on my face was amazement. Keme breathed another of those silent laughs as he adjusted the icepack again.

"Stop teasing them," Indira said. And then, to us, "I'm very happy you two have worked things out."

That seemed like a generous description of what had happened—as far as I could tell, me simply existing had driven Keme to the brink of murder, and then, by hurting my shoulder, I'd won him over completely. Best friends, I thought. And next, roommates.

Before I could voice any of those thoughts, though, I caught a glimpse of Keme's face: the unabashed pleasure at Indira's words, the genuine happiness there. I decided to keep my opinions to myself and said, "Me too."

"The matching tattoos could be of a dolphin wrestling a whale," Fox said. "On your face."

"I think we'll wait on the tattoos. That might raise some questions when I go in for my next job interview."

"Oh, don't do that. That sounds terrible."

"What do you mean?" Millie asked. "You have a job. You're going to stay here and live in Hemlock House and write books."

"A few problems with that," I said. "First, I've hit a dry spell with the writing, which was kind of the whole reason I came here. And second, I think there's still someone out there trying to—I don't know. Frame me. Kill me."

"But if Keme is your roommate—"

That made me do a mental double-take. I'd thought she'd been joking. Keme caught the look on my face and gave me a slanting smile.

"You should get a gun," Fox said. "How many guns do you have?"

"You hate guns," Indira said.

"I really don't think I want a gun," I said.

Fox shrugged. "Deputy Mai has a gun."

I managed to refrain from reminding them that Deputy Mai also had a boyfriend.

"I can borrow my dad's gun," Millie said.

"No!" We all shouted at the same time.

"I don't want to leave," I said, "but honestly, I don't know what else to do. I don't have a job here. I'm sure once they sort out everything with Mr. Huggins, they'll be able to prove I don't really own Hemlock House. I've got nowhere to live. And I've got a murderer who's still focused on me for some reason. The last one seems like a really good reason to take a permanent vacation from Hastings Rock."

Millie looked like she was about to cry. "But you're our friend. We can figure it out. We can find whoever killed Vivienne, and then you'll be safe."

Keme resettled the ice pack. Hard. Kind of like he was hitting me with it. When I started to protest, his glare stopped me. I took the nonverbal message and tried to go for accommodating. "I don't know who we have left. I mean, there's Pippi; she had a motive, I think, but I don't know how we'd prove she managed to get inside Vivienne's room and kill her."

"It's not Pippi," Fox said.

"It's not?" I asked.

Fox shook their head.

"But the story. She had a secret she wanted to cover up—she was paying Vivienne to write a bestseller for her."

"Oh, I don't doubt that. But have you ever read one of Pippi's books?"

"Well, no."

Indira laughed. When I looked at her, she said, "I honestly didn't think about it that way."

"What way?"

"Pippi's books always end the same way," Fox said. "She's always got this thirtysomething female protagonist who loves cupcakes or loves knitting or loves tea—"

"I saw the ones about tea."

"—and they bumble around, spending most of the time talking to their friends about relationship problems, or worrying about relationship problems, or baking cupcakes, or picking out yarn for a special, uh, yarn thing, or steeping tea—"

"Fox," I said.

"Right. Well, every book, she apparently realizes she has to actually solve the mystery that her characters are nominally trying to solve, and so at the end, the bad guy walks onstage and tries to kill the cupcake girl, and that's all the proof the police need. Oh, she always survives, in case you were worried."

"I was not." But something about what Fox had said made my brain stir and stretch. I couldn't put my finger on it, not yet, but it was there, itching at me. Like Indira's question: why now.

"Now, if it were Vivienne's books," Fox continued, "there'd be some kind of twist—and she usually had good ones. The killer would have amnesia. Or the victim would have amnesia. Oh! Or the real killer would be dead the whole time."

I wish I could say I was a deductive genius. I wish I could say I carefully assembled the evidence until all the pieces fit. I wish I could say I was the perfect detective like Will Gower. But writers' brains—at least, this writer's brain—didn't work that way. My brain worked in fits and starts, in intuitive leaps, and all of a sudden, I knew what had happened. The way I had known those (okay, admittedly few) times when a story had come together for me. Vivienne's empty bank accounts. Mr. Huggins's murder. The intruder. Even the food missing from the cellar.

"I know this is going to be asking a lot," I said over Fox. "But I need your help. And it's going to be dangerous."

No one said anything. To be fair, they probably didn't know what to say—or what I was talking about. And then Keme, with a small smile, rapped me on the head in the universal sign for dummy.

CHAPTER 14

After giving everyone their instructions, I went to the den and started to work.

The room felt cold, the air salty and damp and hinting at old paper. I knew that the person who had been in my room had come in here. And while Deputy Bobby's explanations had been sensible and reasonable and, well, sane, I knew that whoever I had been chasing, they had come in here. And they hadn't left through the window.

Since the fireplace seemed to be a dead end, I went to work on the bookshelves. I checked each book, one by one. I had a hunch, but I wanted to be thorough (I hadn't decided yet if the latest iteration of Will Gower would be thorough or would trust his gut). It took me a couple of hours before I found it, and wouldn't you know it—it was a copy of *The Nightingale Murders*, Vivienne's Pulitzer-nominated true crime account of how she had helped the police catch Matrika Nightingale. It wasn't a real book—in so many ways. When I pulled on it, something clicked, and a section of the built-in bookcase swung open to reveal another secret passage.

I grabbed the flashlight that Indira had loaned me and turned it on. I thought about trying 911 again, but in the chaos surrounding the sheriff's death, nobody seemed to have time for what was, admittedly, a wild story. My calls to Deputy Bobby went straight to voicemail. With no other option, I started my phone recording and put it in my pocket. I eased the secret door open all the way. A steep staircase headed down into the dark. That made sense; when I'd been in the cellar, it had seemed small compared to the size of Hemlock House. That's because it *was* small, of course. Because there were other parts of the basement that were secret. Like this one.

As I started down the steps, the beam from my flashlight bounced around. I tried to steady my hand and didn't have much luck. I focused, instead, on breathing. Slow, even breaths. The darkness closed around me as the light from the den grew weaker and weaker, and ahead of me, the flashlight only picked out more steps. I tried to go quietly, but every movement seemed unbearably loud: the whisper of my soles against the treads, the rustle of my clothing. The air was even colder than it had been in the den, and I wished I'd taken Deputy Bobby's advice and put on something besides the SEGA tee and sleep shorts.

When I reached the bottom of the stairs, I could sense that the darkness opened up into a larger space—a room of some sort. I played the flashlight around and saw more shelves built into the walls, loaded with curios under cloches and books and—I tried to step back and smacked into a wall. An enormous taxidermy owl stared back at me, beak open in a silent screech. When I'd swallowed my heart again, I said a few words you can't put in a birthday card.

The flashlight's beam showed me a table and chairs, almost like this was some kind of subterranean parlor, and then a corridor extended off into the gloom. I could make out at least one door. The air smelled like dry, dusty stone, with a hint of something else—kerosene, maybe. And processed food, something that made me think of off-brand spaghetti rings. In the silence, I could hear my blood in my ears.

Without any better options, I started off down the corridor. I swept the flashlight back and forth. The stonework looked old, and so did the furniture in that strange little parlor, and so did the doors. All of this, I was fairly sure, had been part of the house's original design. Nathaniel Blackwood's dream for Hemlock House. Secrets within secrets. I wondered why. Maybe, for a man of his time, even a secret lair needed somewhere to drink tea. Actually, maybe that was still a good rule of thumb.

The first door that I opened revealed a small bedroom. These furnishings were all original too—dark, heavy wood, thick rugs. Not quite as elegant as the main house, but definitely a cut above your modern-day prepper's cot and military-issue blanket. A can of ravioli and red sauce sat on the nightstand next to a modern camping lantern, and a kerosene heater had been pulled close to the bed. Too close for this guy's liking, actually. The room was still warm. My heart started to beat a little faster.

I shut the door and continued down the hall. When I opened the next door, I found Vivienne.

She lay on the floor, on her side, her back to me, but I knew it was her. In a baggy sweatshirt and leggings, she looked small and frail, and it was hard to tell if she was breathing. It looked like she'd been kept prisoner down here since her apparent death. My hand felt greasy around the flashlight. I had a flashback to thirteen-year-old Dash, and for an instant, I knew with terrifying certainty that as soon as I started to speak, my voice would crack.

But somehow, I managed to say, "Vivienne? It's me, Dash. Dashiell. Jonny and Patricia's son." She didn't respond. I crossed the room to her. The stillness and the dark felt like a weight bearing down on me, and it was surprisingly difficult to raise my voice. "Vivienne? Can you hear me? Are you all right?" I reached out to touch her shoulder.

She rolled over more quickly than I expected, and a gun came up, pointed right in my face. "You stupid boy," Vivienne said. "You've ruined everything."

CHAPTER 15

I stared at the gun. I wanted to move my eyes to Vivienne's face, but I couldn't. The gun was like a magnet, and I couldn't pull my eyes away from it.

"Listen to me very carefully," Vivienne said. Her words were clipped. "Put the flashlight down."

I put the flashlight down, and it rolled away on the uneven floor. The light warped along Vivienne. For a moment, it ballooned along the side of her face. And then she was in shadow, and the gun was a glint of blued steel.

"Take one step back. One, Dashiell. I'll shoot you if you try to run."

I took a step back. And somehow, I managed to say, "Just Dash."

"Just Dash," she mimicked as she got up. "Hardly. You're not *just* anything. Do you know how carefully I've planned? How hard I worked? And you still managed to bring the whole thing crashing down."

As my eyes adjusted, I got a better look at her. The strain of the last few days showed in her face: her eyes hollowed out with shadows, her hair a mess. She looked older. Still full of that terrifying vitality, but as though she'd sprung a leak, and it was slowly draining out of her.

"It went wrong," I said, "because—"

"Because that idiot Huggins betrayed me! Precisely!"

"Like you said, you had the whole thing—"

"I had the whole thing planned! Yes, yes! Every bit of it! I was going to disappear. It was going to be as simple as that. I'd be dead, as far as anyone knew. Certainly as far as my dear friends at the Internal Revenue Service knew. Do you know something, Dashiell? A little life lesson, although you won't have time to put it to much use: your bad decisions catch up to you."

"You'd been cheating on—"

"On my taxes!"

I was starting to think I was never going to finish a sentence.

"That idiot Huggins said he'd hired an expert. He said the whole thing was foolproof. He said everyone did it—everyone with money did it. Moved things around. Kept what they'd earned instead of letting the government go at it like a hog at a trough. And then the letters started coming. The notification of an audit. I knew I had to do something, but I figured it could all be handled. I'd tell them Huggins had told me to do it; that seemed a simple enough explanation. I'd pay the fine, whatever it was, and life would go on."

"Except it wasn't just the taxes," I said. "It was Matrika—"

"Nightingale, yes! She ruined everything."

"Okay, but if I could have a turn—"

"Nightingale, with her persistence and her whining and her complaints and her demand that they reopen the case, her appeal for a consideration of new DNA evidence. Well, God help me, we didn't even know about DNA back then. I certainly couldn't have prepared for that, and let me tell you, I tried to prepare for everything."

"Because you—"

"Framed her!"

I said some more of those un-birthday-card-like words under my breath.

"Of course I did," Vivienne continued, gesticulating with the gun. "You're not an idiot, Dashiell, appearances to the contrary. The evidence was there. She made it so easy; she was practically asking for it, the way she left her office unlocked, with all those stupid feathers lying around, everything covered in her fingerprints."

"It worked out perfectly," I said, "except an innocent woman went to prison for the rest of her life, and a serial killer escaped."

"Don't be ridiculous. There never was a serial killer; we came up with that, Adrian and I. We both needed something big, something to help us break out. He was muddling along in the district attorney's office, and I—I knew I could be great if someone would just give me a chance."

"And all it took was ruining Matrika Nightingale's life."

"I hadn't thought about her in years, can you believe that? The letters came. The threats. The pleas. I filed them away in case I ever needed them, but I didn't think about her, not really. And then I learned about the appeal, and I knew it was all going to come undone. Everything I'd worked for. Everything I'd built. But still, I had time to prepare. Appeals are a lengthy process; I didn't need to rush."

"So you decided—"

"To fake my own death. It was the perfect plan. My money was safe and sound in a numbered account in the Caymans. I'd have a tragic accident. The sheriff and the district medical examiner were more than willing to help me on my way, as it were, in exchange for my generous appreciation."

"But Matrika—"

"Escaped! And then there was no time left; I had to run."

"Only you didn't count on—"

"Huggins turning on me like the traitorous snake he was." Vivienne's voice was thick with rage. "He was always nervous. Always high-strung. He thought the Nightingale case would put him in the national spotlight, but as soon as the case went to trial, he fell apart. A complete nervous breakdown. He left the district attorney's office—was practically forced out. Who took care of him? Me. Who made sure he always had a roof over his head, food to eat? Me. And how did he show his gratitude? He came here as soon as he learned about the appeal, and he told me he was going to tell them it was my idea. It took everything I had to persuade him that things would be all right. We'd already laid the groundwork for me to disappear; we simply had to accelerate the timeline. Once I was established, I'd make arrangements for him to join me. Everything would have been fine."

"When did you realize that Mr. Huggins had stolen your money?"

Her laugh sounded startled more than amused. "Almost immediately. My arrangements with the sheriff went off perfectly: the corpse from the morgue, which he quickly made disappear into a body bag; the deal with the district medical examiner; all of it. I was free. Except when I retrieved my new ID and account information, I couldn't access any of the money. I thought something was wrong. I thought there had been a mistake. And then Adrian came here and told me what he'd done. All of my money in a numbered account, and I couldn't get it because he was the only one who had the number. He was so smug. He thought he was so smart. He stood there, telling me how he'd taken everything, how he was the one who deserved it. He was going to kill me, he said; he was going to make sure everyone thought you'd done it." Her voice tightened. "But Adrian was always weak. He hesitated. And he didn't expect me to be armed. Or to be ready to defend myself. But he should have remembered that I've dealt with far more dangerous men than Adrian Huggins."

"You were stuck here," I said. "Looking for the account numbers. That's why you tore apart Mr. Huggins's house. And that's why you went back again last night. You were the one the sheriff was talking to when I was upstairs. He wasn't surprised to see you; he was the one who helped you fake your own death. That's why he was so lax about procedure. He even had authority to remove your 'body' from the scene."

"Yes, well, he'd become a loose thread," Vivienne said with a grimace. "It was one thing to help me disappear, but I knew he wouldn't look away after what I'd done to Adrian. He had to go. And can you imagine my luck? Matrika was right there, a perfect patsy for the deputies to pick up. God, the poor thing really has no luck. Can you believe I managed to get away with it twice?"

"You haven't gotten away with it yet."

"Almost, Dashiell. One more loose end. And then, money or no money, I'll be gone. It's not personal, by the way. I didn't expect you to find my body. I didn't really think about you at all—it was simply poor timing, you being here. I thought—"

"You thought I'd be useful," I said. "Because your writing had stalled. You told me when we first met that you knew what writer's block felt like. You ripped off Pippi's cozy because you thought it might help, but you must have known it was too different from your own style. And then I wandered into your life." In the grand scheme, the hurt I felt about my writing was a small thing, and my reaction was probably childish. But I couldn't quite keep the ache out of my voice when I said, "You told me how much you liked 'Murder on the Emerald Express.'"

In the distance, waves beat against the cliffs. I thought I could hear her fingers open and close around the gun's grip.

"You should be flattered, Dashiell. I would have stolen your work, of course, but isn't that the highest form of flattery?"

"No. Not really."

"It was a risk, searching your room when I knew you were in the house. But I did hope that you'd managed to find something at Adrian's house, something I'd missed. If there was even the slightest chance..."

"I did, actually. I found his files from the Nightingale murders. That's really when it all started to come together, even though I didn't realize it at the time."

"Ah." It was difficult to tell under the thick shadows, but Vivienne's face seemed to change, and her voice was different when she said, "I think it's time for us to take a walk, Dashiell. Turn around and slowly—slowly—exit the room."

I turned—slowly—and headed out of the room.

"Left," Vivienne said.

So, I turned left.

She was clever. She was wily. She had faced down killers of all kinds over the course of her life, and she'd always come out on top. Because she was Vivienne Carver. She didn't make any stupid mistakes like walking too close to me. She didn't give me a chance to catch her by surprise, to feign a stumble, to wrest the gun away. If I made a wrong move, she'd kill me, and that would be that.

The corridor ended in a half-flight of stairs that led up to an old door, barely more than a shape in the thick shadows. When I reached it, I caught a whiff of dry rot and then fresh, briny air.

"Open it," Vivienne said. "And if you're thinking about running, think again."

The door was heavy, and it took a strong pull to get it moving. As it inched open, moonlight and the roar of the waves spilled into the dark stillness of the tunnel.

"It will look like an accident," Vivienne said over the noise. When I looked back, the ambient light fell over her face: the eyes, the flattened hair, the small, hard mouth. "If that's any consolation."

As I stepped out into the night, it didn't seem like a consolation. The door hidden in the foundation—invisible from the outside—opened onto the rocky strip of cliff behind Hemlock House. The hemlocks grew thick and tangled here, warped by decades of storms into gnarled embraces. The wind ripped at my hair and sent the leaves whispering, the branches clattering. I could taste salt in my mouth, and something else that I thought was pure fear.

"The cliff!" Vivienne shouted behind me. "Go!"

I took a stumbling step into the shifting shadows under the hemlocks, and I turned to face her. The gun was steady in her hands; it seemed like the only thing that wasn't moving—the hemlocks swaying, the breeze pulling at my tee, even the ground underfoot slippery with spray.

"You don't have to do this," I said. "You don't have to kill me."

"I'm sorry, Dashiell, but I think I do. And I'm sure, as a writer yourself, you can appreciate the irony. All those years of catching murderers, and now I'm going to get away with it myself."

"It's just Dash," I said.

For a moment, incomprehension showed in her eyes.

"I prefer Dash," I said. "I told you that."

She opened her mouth.

"Did you all hear her?" I asked.

"Loud and clear," Fox called from one side of the house. They poked their head out, their face grim.

Millie emerged from the other side, her usually cheery complexion set in a furious scowl. "We heard EVERYTHING!"

Vivienne actually jumped a little at the volume. I said a little prayer of thanks that Fox had spoken first, or I'd probably have a sizable hole in me.

"What is this?" Vivienne asked. And then, with a disbelieving laugh, "A public confession. Good God, isn't that the oldest trick in the book?"

"Put the gun down, Vivienne," Fox said. "We were your friends. This doesn't have to get any worse."

Vivienne's mouth tightened into a line. The waves turned and broke. The wind rushed through the trees. Over Hemlock House, a star was falling—a glimmer, and then gone. And whatever I'd seen in Vivienne's face, for a single instant, was gone too. Now it had only a burned-out coldness.

"I don't think so," Vivienne said. "Come with me. We'll take a different route. There are other ways out of Hemlock House."

"I don't think so," I said.

"Come with me or I'll shoot you this instant, you stupid—"

The bong sounded like something out of a cartoon. Vivienne's eyes rolled up in her head, and she did a staggering foxtrot to the left, and then she crumpled. Behind her, Keme held a massive cast-iron pan, and his face was set with disturbingly cold intent.

The only thing I could come up with was "Keme!"

Indira appeared from the tunnel under Hemlock House. She stepped around Keme carrying a length of rope, and she knelt and began tying Vivienne's hands—although, to be fair, it looked like Keme had knocked Vivienne into next year, so I wasn't sure the ropes were really necessary.

"Keme had very strong opinions about certain parts of your plan," Indira said. "He told me about them. At length."

"He did?"

Keme made a rude gesture at me. Then, the corner of his mouth cracked into a smile.

"It was either let him help," Indira continued, "or spend the rest of the night arguing with him."

"But—that wasn't the plan. Keme was supposed to be safely somewhere else. Anywhere else. And you were supposed to call the sheriff's office while I kept her busy."

"Yes, well, Keme was feeling quite…protective."

Keme looked like he was feeling seventeen years old and chock full of testosterone—and, frankly, like he wanted to do some more bashing with that frying pan. I thought one of us should probably take it away from him before he decided to indulge himself.

"Wait," I said. "He was feeling protective of me?"

Indira and Keme shared a look, and then Keme stared straight at me and rolled his eyes.

A laugh that was somewhere between mania and hysteria bubbled up inside me.

Millie's cry of "BOBBY!" interrupted me before I could completely fall apart.

And there he was: Deputy Bobby in his khaki uniform, staring down at us, apparently speechless. And then, with what sounded like a lot of effort, he said, "What in the world is going on?"

CHAPTER 16

A few days later, Keme and I were playing Fortnite in the billiard room (which was really more of a family room, but the name was too cool to change), and I was getting slaughtered. I mean, I wasn't bad. But Keme was in a league of his own.

"Wait, wait, wait—" I tried.

But Keme's protectiveness had either been temporary or did not extend to the realm of video games. He didn't even have the decency to talk crap; he just gave me a pitying look, killed me, and kept playing.

After that night with Vivienne, I'd been in a weird limbo. Deputy Bobby had arrested Vivienne—which didn't take the first time, on account of the fact that Keme had sparked her out with kitchenware. More deputies had come. The chief deputy, who was also the acting sheriff—a terrifyingly reserved woman named Acosta—had come. And we'd all ended up at the station, telling our story. Acosta—and, for that matter, Deputy Bobby—had shared their thoughts about our plan (to borrow Indira's phrase, they'd shared their thoughts *at length*). But say what you will about an engineered public confession, it's a classic for a reason, especially when you record it.

Since then, there'd been a few follow-up interviews, but my days, for the most part, had been calm and quiet. And, frankly, a little empty. Which was where Keme came in—maybe he'd sensed I needed some company, or maybe

Indira had said something after the third chocolate cake I devoured. We played video games. And we hung out. And the best part was that with Keme, I didn't have to talk. I saved all my talking for Fox, who came by to eat Indira's cooking, and Millie, who was at Hemlock House whenever she wasn't working.

A tap at the window interrupted another round of Keme ruthlessly hunting me down and exterminating me. Deputy Bobby was looking in at us, shading his eyes with one hand. I dropped the controller, ignored the look that Keme gave me—it was, for a teenager, a surprisingly knowing look—and motioned to Deputy Bobby that I'd meet him on the terrace.

When I let myself outside, the day was bright, and a clear, blue sky stretched as far as I could see. The sun was warm, and the air was sweet with the smell of rain-washed grass and hemlock and rose. Deputy Bobby appeared a moment later. He wasn't in uniform, I saw—a hoodie, joggers, and these suspiciously cool sneakers that were like another window into Deputy Bobby.

"Was that Fortnite?" he asked as he stepped up onto the terrace.

"You play?"

"Why were you trying to climb that tree?"

"I wasn't trying to climb it; I got stuck—" I caught his hint of a smile. "Don't start with me! I already have to put up with this kind of abuse from Keme."

"It was cute when you were trying to snipe."

Cute, I thought. But I said, "You try playing with him. He's a one-man assassination squad."

That made Deputy Bobby grin. He relaxed against the parapet and folded his arms. "No shorts? No T-shirt?"

I plucked at my hoodie, but I said, "It doesn't make any sense. It's warm. It's sunny! Why am I still cold?"

His grin got wider. "You finally look like a local."

"Just in time, huh?"

He cocked his head, and his grin dimmed a little. "What's that mean?"

"I don't know."

A gull called.

"Are you leaving?"

I shrugged.

Deputy Bobby considered me. "I heard Acosta talked to you about Hemlock House."

"Talked to me is a very good way of putting it. Obviously I can't inherit anything from Vivienne because she's alive, so that part doesn't matter, but the sheriff told me that, as far as anyone can tell, I really am the legal owner of Hemlock House. According to the county recorder, a quitclaim deed was filed by Vivienne Carver—signed and notarized, everything above board—giving me full ownership of the property. Then Acosta told me she didn't believe for a minute that Vivienne had signed that deed, and I'd better prepare myself for a legal battle."

"Maybe."

"What maybe? She's going to want her house back."

"She's got a lot to worry about. Not just the murders—"

"And attempted murder. That part is very important to me."

"—but also everything with the Nightingale murders. Matrika is back at the state penitentiary, and there will be consequences for the escape, but her appeal is going to move forward."

"And she'll be cleared by the DNA," I said. "Eventually."

"She's also going to sue Vivienne for everything she owns," Deputy Bobby said. "So, Vivienne might not be in a rush to get Hemlock House back. As it stands, she barely has the funds to hire a defense lawyer—I can't imagine she wants to extend herself and try a civil suit at the same time. Besides, she's too busy trying to blame everything on Huggins—it's a real song and dance, considering she's spent the last thirty years putting herself in the spotlight and Huggins is dead."

"Kind of puts a damper on all those thirtieth anniversary 'Where are they now' specials, doesn't it?"

But Deputy Bobby didn't smile. He had his usual Deputy Bobby earnestness as he said, "What I'm trying to say is Hemlock House is yours, if you want it."

"I guess."

The gull again. And the restlessness of the ocean.

"You know," Deputy Bobby said, "a lot of people would be thrilled to have a mansion fall into their laps. Especially one that's completely paid off. Especially if they're a talented writer looking for a place where they can work in peace and quiet."

"You haven't heard Millie after she's worked a morning shift at Chipper and had unlimited access to the espresso. Peace and quiet it is not."

"Especially if it's a good town, with good people. Especially if they've got friends who care about them and want them to be happy. Especially if everyone wants them to stay."

"I want to loop back to the part about me being talented."

"Funny. I wanted to talk some more about how I feel about you almost getting yourself killed so you could trick Vivienne into a confession."

"Never mind. I decided I'm fine with letting the conversation move forward."

But it didn't. It stalled right then, and Deputy Bobby was looking at me with those eyes like burnished bronze, and I couldn't hear the ocean anymore, couldn't hear the gulls, couldn't hear the breeze that ruffled his hair.

"I brought you something," he said. "In case you decide to stay."

"Oh yeah?" (I'm a writer, ladies and gentlemen. Words are my stock-in-trade.)

He headed for his car, and over his shoulder, he tossed back, "I put it in the coach house. It's for your own good, Mr. Dane."

"I prefer Dash."

That goofy grin exploded as he swung himself up into the Pilot. "I know."

And then he shut the door, and a moment later, he was driving away.

I went to the coach house.

There was a familiar-looking envelope on the windshield of the Jeep: another ticket from Deputy Bobby. Only, when I opened it, it wasn't a ticket. It was a warning for expired tags. And then, in handwriting that was quickly becoming familiar, *I can't give you a ticket because it's parked on private property. Please, for the love of God, help me out here.*

But that wasn't the gift. The gift was a bike.

It was a cute little fixed-gear with a blue frame, clearly used, and my guess was that it had been Deputy Bobby's, or maybe West's. He'd tied a bow on it with white ribbon, and if Deputy Bobby wasn't actually a straight boy, that incredibly terrible bow made me think you'd have to squint to tell the difference. I realized I was smiling, and I couldn't seem to wipe it off my face.

The rap of knuckles on wood broke the moment. Behind me, Keme leaned through the doorway, his expression expectant. He tilted his head back toward the house and our game.

"Actually—" I gave the bike another look. "—I think I'm going to finish unpacking."

DUDE MAGNET

Keep reading for a sneak preview of *Dude Magnet*, the next book in The Last Picks.

CHAPTER 1

"I think we might possibly, maybe, have made a mistake," I said.

At the top of Hemlock House's grand staircase, the bride-to-be asked, "What about this ceiling? Could we smash it out?"

My friends looked to me for a response.

The Last Picks—as Fox had told me, they called themselves that because they were always the last picks in gym (and for pretty much everything else)—were here today because: a) they were almost always here, and b) they were providing emotional support, and c) this was all Millie's fault. (As a side note, I definitely fell into that "last picks" category too.) There were five of us: Millie, who was like a tiny blond version of a caffeinated Energizer bunny. Indira, with her laugh lines and that lone shock of white hair like a witch. Fox, their graying hair buzzed—today, under a top hat that featured little gears and welding goggles, and which didn't go with what they had told me (at length) was called a seductress blouse. And Keme, short and lean and tan from a summer of surfing, his long hair pushed behind his ears.

"Oh my God," Millie whisper-screamed (unhelpfully). "They're so in love! Isn't this the cutest? This is the CUTEST!"

"Mom," the groom-to-be shouted down the stairs. "Can we do something about this ceiling?"

"The cutest," Fox murmured. They sounded like someone trying to pick out their favorite knife.

Keme didn't quite make a growling noise, but he folded his arms—audibly—and set his jaw as he stared at the happy couple.

"Tell them no." Indira nudged me. "Tell them they can't make any alterations."

"Why me?" I asked.

The groom's mother and father and grandmother were making their way up the stairs now: Mom on her phone. Dad panting. Grandma testing each step by hammering down with the ferrule of her cane.

"Because it's your house," Millie said unhelpfully.

"Because I already had to stop them with the wallpaper," Fox said with a definite tone.

Keme gave me a look that translated to: *Don't be such a wuss.*

"Because this was your idea," Indira said.

I gaped at them. "This was Millie's idea!"

Millie nodded enthusiastically and then said, "I bet her dress is going to be gorgeous."

There wasn't much doubt about that since the Gauthier-Meadows clan, who were currently occupying my grand staircase, had Scrooge McDuck kind of money. And I needed money. The thing about suddenly coming into possession of a Class V haunted mansion? (Well, one of the things, anyway.) They cost a lot of money. Buckets of money. Even when they're in great condition, like Hemlock House. And since I was still, uh, brainstorming my brilliant masterpiece of a novel that would doubtless bring me instant fame and fortune, and since I had no employable skills, I needed to do something. Also, in Millie's (and, I suppose, my) defense, the idea had sounded like a good one. Hemlock House—with its wainscotting and damask wallpaper and antique Chesterfields and curios and, most importantly, books—was beautiful. It was enormous. And it was one of those rare period homes that had survived into the twenty-first century relatively unscathed. Combined with the scenery of the

Oregon Coast at its peak in early September, it was a picture-perfect place for a wedding. Or so Millie and I had claimed in the online ads.

We had not accounted for things like, I don't know, acoustics.

The bride-to-be tilted her head back and belted out a note.

Millie winced.

Keme covered his ears.

Fox said, "It's like someone stuffed a cat inside a set of bagpipes."

"It's a travesty," Indira said.

"It's the acoustics," the bride-to-be announced. "They're all wrong."

Even the groom-to-be looked like he was having a bit of trouble swallowing that explanation. A laugh from farther down the hall made me glance over. The groom-to-be's twin was leaning against a piece of gorgeous period furniture that Indira insisted on calling a commode. (I refused to call it that.) Next to him, the maid of honor (to be?) was covering a grin.

"Mom," the groom-to-be said. "The ceiling?"

"I'll call a contractor," she said without looking up from her phone.

Fox hissed.

Indira shoved me forward.

The sound of my steps must have drawn their attention, because every eye turned toward me. Mom even deigned to look up from her phone.

"Uh, you know," I said. "About the house."

"You can't rip out the ceiling," Fox prompted in a whisper.

"Why not?" the grandmother asked. "We'll pay for it."

"Well," I said.

Apparently, they wanted more than that.

The twin looked like he was trying not to laugh again.

"It's not so much the money," I said, "as it is that you, um, can't."

"What's he saying?" the bride-to-be asked. "I don't understand what he's saying."

"It's a historic house," I said. "And the contract clearly says no alterations."

"But the acoustics," the bride-to-be wailed. "My head. Baby, I'm getting a headache."

"Why's it such a big deal?" Dad asked. He was too loud, and it didn't go well with his rounded shoulders and potbelly. "It's a house. And we said we'd pay."

Mom gave him a freezing glance and said, "Get the contract, Gary."

Gary grimaced at her; it took me a moment to realize it was supposed to be a smile. He scurried down the steps, darted past us—with a glare for me—and disappeared outside.

"Sharian," Fox said, "why don't we talk about the reception? Millie, come on."

"And Mrs. Meadows," Indira said, "I wanted to go over a few of the dietary restrictions your guests noted."

The double distractions broke the tension of the moment. Sharian (the bride-to-be) dragged Mason (the groom-to-be) down the stairs, and they followed Fox and Millie into the living room. Indira moved to join Mom and Grandma, where they began to confer.

Keme hadn't abandoned me, although he was giving me a look that mingled disappointment and amusement.

"Fine," I said. "Next time, you can tell them."

He rolled his eyes and headed toward the kitchen.

"Hey."

The voice came from behind me, and I turned. It was the twin, Cole. He and his brother were unobjectionably handsome: dark hair, dark eyes, athletic builds even though they were going into their thirties. Mason (the groom-to-be) wore his hair in a side part with waves, and he looked every bit the high-achieving son of a fantabulously wealthy family, aside from a coconut-bead necklace—which felt like a lame bit of leftover teenagery. Cole (aka Trouble) wore his hair shorter, although it was hard to name a specific style since he looked like he'd woken up. Under a bridge. After a seriously rough night. The joggers and hoodie weren't helping his case; they must have been expensive, but they looked lived-in, to put it generously.

"Hi," I said.

"You're cute." He leaned against a console table. It rocked, and a porcelain vase wobbled. Cole said a word you're not supposed to say in front of your grandma and caught the vase (barely). Then he looked at me.

"Excuse me," I said. "I've got to check on a few things."

Which was a total lie. But I did walk purposefully toward the den and open the door and stand there, hands on hips, pretending to scrutinize something. Through the window, I had a good line of sight to Gary (father-of-the-groom), who was currently vaping and playing a game on his phone. I thought it was a calculated risk; Becky (mother-of-the-groom) did not seem like the kind of woman who tolerated loafing around.

"Okay," Trouble (aka Cole) said behind me, "that was embarrassing."

Trying not to sigh, I turned around. Again.

"I was trying to look cool," he said with a grin.

"I liked the part at the end where you almost broke an irreplaceable vase."

His grin got bigger. "That wasn't my favorite part, actually."

"Uh huh."

"My favorite part was when I told you how cute you are."

I rolled my eyes. Loudly.

That made him burst out laughing. He stepped in, closing the distance between us, and all of a sudden Keme was there. Keme had to be five or six inches shorter than this guy, and although Keme was definitely stronger than he looked—cue one humiliating bout of Millie-inspired wrestling—he was still a teenager (a teenager, it must be noted, who was perpetually hungry, ate everything Indira put in front of him, and still looked like he'd disappear if he turned sideways). Cole probably had thirty pounds on him, and those thirty pounds were muscle.

None of it slowed Keme down. He put himself between us, hand on Cole's chest, and shoved. Cole took a surprised step back and said, "Whoa."

Keme glowered at him.

"It's all right," I said, touching Keme's arm. The boy's whole body was tight with a kind of fight-or-flight energy; Keme was practically buzzing with it. I'd never seen him like this before. "It's okay," I said in a softer voice. "We were talking."

Keme shook his head at my words and then pointed to his eye and then to Cole. It was getting easier to understand Keme, although I still wished he'd talk (Indira insisted he was perfectly able to, but I'd never heard a word from him).

I tried to interpret his gesture. "You've got your eye on him—"

Keme shook his head and pointed to his eye again.

Then I saw it. "Oh. He's high."

Cole laughed and rubbed the back of his neck. "Not, like, super high. Just enough to float through this. Sorry, did I do something wrong?"

"No," I said. I squeezed Keme's arm and got him moving. "I'm sorry about the confusion. Are you okay?"

"Yeah, of course—"

"Great. Excuse us."

I steered Keme into what was called the north lobby (because in a place like Hemlock House, even weird little side pockets needed their own special names). Voice low, I asked, "What's going on?"

Keme wouldn't look at me.

"Hey. Mister."

Slowly, he dragged his eyes to my face. His arm was still tense under my hand. He set his jaw.

After a deep breath, I said, "Thank you."

A hint of confusion showed in his eyes.

"For caring," I said. "And for being worried."

He shrugged.

"But," I said.

He tried to pull free.

I held on. "But," I said again, "you can't go around pushing people and—"

Keme yanked his arm away and, before I could stop him, pushed through the door to the servants' dining room. A moment later, a second door slammed, and I knew he'd left Hemlock House in true teenager fashion.

"Everything okay?"

That was Trouble with a capital T again.

"Do you always sneak up behind people?" I asked.

The smile made him look younger. "I'm off my game today."

The maid of honor was watching us from down the hall, and she looked like she was enjoying every minute of this agony.

"Can we start over?" Cole asked.

"I don't have an unlimited supply of vases."

He grinned and said, "Hi, I'm Cole."

"You look familiar. I think I've seen you before."

"Nope, that was my twin. I'm way better looking."

"Uh huh."

"It's easy to tell us apart. For example, I'm a lefty. I know for a fact that Taylor Swift is a million times better than Beyonce, I've got way better handwriting, I never wear red because that was the only color my mom let me wear when I was growing up, and Mason is a total lightweight when it comes to, uh, certain substances."

"You're losing me," I told him.

"I've definitely got a better sense of humor, I'm not a corporate sellout, oh, yeah, and I've got these little freckles in a certain spot." He gave me the grin again. "But I need to know you a little better before I show you."

"Cute."

"See? I think you're cute. You think I'm cute. We're a match."

In spite of myself, I laughed. "Let's keep this strictly professional."

"God, no. That sounds terrible. Can I take you to dinner?"

I made a noise and slid around him.

Cole moved with me, stepping into my path. "Please let me take you to dinner."

"I've got to work."

"We can go whenever you're done. I'm a bum and a loser, to quote my parents, so I'm at your beck and call."

"There's a million things to do before the wedding."

"But you have to eat sometime, right? What if I pick up food and bring it over?"

I tried to slide around him again.

He moved with me again. "Please? It's dinner. I'll be a perfect gentleman." He held up two fingers. "I won't even get high."

"I think the Scouts do three fingers."

"But you knew what I was going for! See how in sync we are?"

That made me laugh again.

I almost said no. But he had a great smile: big and bright and wide. And I'd always liked confident guys. And, if I had a gun to my head, I could admit I was, well, lonely.

Not *lonely* lonely. I mean, I had Millie and Fox and Indira and Keme—they were the best thing to happen to me in a long time. They were my friends. We were the Last Picks, and I loved spending time with them. But friends or no friends, the transition from a long-term, serious relationship to being totally, absolutely, unrelentingly single hadn't been easy. I missed quiet nights staying in with my person. I missed the easiness of casual touch. I missed intimacy—not sex, but, yeah, that too. And while I wasn't under any delusions that Mr. Trouble with a capital T was going to be my one true love, he seemed sweet and fun and unexpectedly earnest. He'd already made me laugh twice; that was a good sign, right?

"What are your parents going to say?"

"Oh God, they've known we're bi for, like, ever."

"Not what I meant."

"If I skip all the pre-wedding festivities? I'm a constant disappointment. They'd be worried if I didn't screw things up."

"That's not as encouraging as you think."

"I feel like you're about to say yes."

"Dinner," I said.

His grin lit up his face.

I held up a finger. "Only dinner."

"I told you: I'm a perfect gentleman."

"Who's also a perpetual disappointment."

"Well, yeah," he said. He had a dimple, I realized. An extremely dangerous dimple. "Have you met my family? So, if I could get your number…"

As I finished rattling off digits, raised voices erupted in the living room. Cole's expression changed to resignation, and I slipped past him (successfully, this time) to return to the hall.

The pocket doors to the living room were open, and the family was clustered around Mason (the groom-to-be) in a shouting scrum: Becky (Mom), Gary (Dad), Sharian (the bride-to-be), and Jodi (Grandma).

"What are you talking about?" Gary boomed. "You're out of your mind."

Becky said something that, once you cleaned it up, was something along the lines of "Are you an idiot?"

Sharian was wailing, "I don't understand. I don't understand."

"It's my money," Mason said. "That's what the trust says. It's mine once I turn thirty-one. I can do whatever I want with it."

"But I don't understand," Sharian said. "My head. Oh my God, my head, I'm going to be sick."

"There's nothing to understand," Mason said. "I'm giving it away to charity. All of it. End of conversation. It's mine, and I can do whatever I want—"

Mason's grandmother slapped him. The crack of the blow silenced everyone. Mason shook his head; to judge by the look in his eyes, he'd never been hit before. The grandmother raised her hand like she might hit him again, but instead, she spoke, her voice low and controlled and furious. "It is my money, you stupid, selfish boy."

No one said anything for what felt like a long time. No one moved. No one breathed.

"I'm going to be sick," Sharian moaned again. She took a tottering step. "Penny? Where's Penny?"

That was when I noticed the maid of honor was missing.

Next to me, Cole let out a harsh breath. His cheeks were flushed, and his hands were trembling; he tried hiding them in his pockets, but the first time, he couldn't get them in. He didn't even seem to realize I was still there as he said to himself, "Mase, you moron."

I needed to say something. I needed to suggest we take a break. Maybe everyone needed some space.

But as I opened my mouth, something impossible happened.

A man walked into the hall. He looked impeccably handsome: square jawed, swooshy haired, that strong nose that he didn't like, but that was, of course, perfect for his face. Cardigan and chinos and boat shoes. He looked like he'd fallen out of a different time, a different place—somewhere, undoubtedly, with a lot more money.

He glanced around the hall, confusion scrawled across those yacht club features, and then his eyes settled on me. The old, familiar smile spread across his face, and for a moment, I forgot how it had ended.

"Dash!" he called out.

"Uh, hi, Hugo."

ACKNOWLEDGEMENTS

My deepest thanks go out to the following people (in alphabetical order):

Jolanta Benal, for Humphrey vs. Humphry, Mr. Huggings, and for reminding me there's no room at the inn.

Savannah Cordle, for keeping track of who's saying what, for helping me think more carefully about the first chapter, and for all her kind comments about these dummies.

Fritz, for his help proofing the text, for spotting my messed-up pronouns (it always happens somehow!), and for pointing out that people might want to know where Hastings Rock is.

Austin Gwin, for his help with Providence vs. Portsmouth, for the clarification about Will Gower, and for his general encouragement about what has been an exciting but also scary new project.

Marie Lenglet, for catching all those missing Deputy Bobbies, for her wonderful insights into how to make this cozier (the library will get better, I promise), and for my terrible gaffe about The Rolling Stones—my only excuse is that I wasn't quite awake yet.

Raj Mangat, for pointing out (quite rightly!) that Dash needs his coffee; for her excellent feedback about Bobby (even if he's still maybe a little too nice), and for asking so many wonderful questions to clarify important elements of the story.

Ravkiran Mangat, for generously jumping in to provide her cozy expertise, and for all her excellent feedback on where the book was falling short and how to make it better.

Cheryl Oakley, for her excellent plot questions about Matrika, for catching my brilliant typos (like the new word I invented: "felts"), and for providing all this excellent feedback after being injured!

Meredith Otto, for asking so many questions—about Vivienne's husband, about Millie's attention span, about our mysterious lumberjack, and more!

Pepe, for proofing the text, for help with my musical references, and for asking that excellent question about Vivienne's forged will.

Nichole Reeder, for her help with proofing the text, for asking excellent questions about time and distance, and for reminding me there were two gunshots (among other things!).

Tray Stephenson, for catching my typos that slipped past everyone else, for his kind words about this new endeavor, and for making me laugh about Millie.

Mark Wallace, for spotting those missing end marks (and other mistakes), for his reader-brain feedback on when the story takes off, and for his kind words about all those moments of authorial intrusion.

Wendy Wickett, for so much excellent editorial feedback, including my missing punctuation and, of course, all the repetitive phrasing.

Special thanks to Crystal and Raye for catching errors in the ARC.

Finally, I'd like to acknowledge two authors whose work has pushed the bounds of the cozy mystery genre and, in doing so, inspired me to try my hand at it. Richard Osman's Thursday Murder Club series showed me that cozy mysteries could engage with difficult (even heartbreaking) realities in an intelligent and authentic way, while still being gentle and, yes, cozy. And Josh Lanyon's Secrets and Scrabble series showed me that cozies could be beautifully written, with compelling, interesting, believable characters—who also happened to be men. I hope my small tributes to Pirate's Cove show how grateful I am for her books.

ABOUT THE AUTHOR

For advanced access, exclusive content, limited-time promotions, and insider information, please sign up for my mailing list at **www.gregoryashe.com**.

Printed in Great Britain
by Amazon

50413474R00101